PRINCE PERFECT

PRINCE PERFECT

Josef Nix

Strategic Book Publishing and Rights Co.

Strategic Book Publishing & Rights Co., LLC
USA | Singapore
www.sbpra.com

For information about special discounts for bulk purchases, please contact Strategic Book Publishing and Rights Co. Special Sales, at bookorder@sbpra.net.

ISBN: 978-1-68181-423-0

To Keith, my very own brown-eyed, handsome man. Thanks for being everything I ever dreamed of and more. I love you.

Once upon a time long ago in a faraway country, there lived a handsome prince...

CHAPTER 1

Mark was a nice Jewish boy, one of those prize catches in our small, isolated community where our matchmaking yentas practiced their ancient craft under the cooling breeze of ceiling fans on magnolia scented screened-in porches while sipping tall glasses of sweet iced tea. Mark's daddy was a fine man, "a big wig in state government." His mother must have chaired just about every committee the temple let women on as well as civic groups from the Junior League even on down. They had a nice home in the best neighborhood, tastefully appointed to showcase Mark's great-great-grandmother's antiques saved from plunder during the siege and occupation. All this was facts-of-life not lost on the drawling dowagers whose self-appointed community responsibilities were to protect the treasures of the Levy family in which Mark figured in line just below the sabre-slashed portrait of his great-great-grandfather in full Confederate officer regalia.

That summer, Mark had just returned from Up North and the yentas had gathered on Mama's porch to discuss the marketability of his Ivy League diploma. With predictable Southern tact, they were sounding Mama out on my sister's current status of eligibility. Mama, ever cautious of running counter of Linda's temper, or as Miz Feinstein put it, her "high spirits," was side-stepping the issue by proffering more of Miz Edna's delicacies.

"Why, Miz Santo, you've not had near enough of Edna's pralines. You know she'll be hurt if you don't eat at least one more."

Miz Santo, acting as yenta-in-chief, was not to be distracted from the business at hand.

"I'm on a diet. Now tell me, just where is that daughter of yours?"

Mama mumbled something non-committal about Linda taking some time off "to travel." Giving no pause for advantage, she continued, calling toward the kitchen where I was making a sandwich.

"Allen! Please bring me a Tupperware™ bowl out here so's I can pack some of Edna's pralines for Miz Santo to take home with her."

I was getting the bowl down while half-heartedly listening to Mama's comments on choices of mate for the Levy Boy. I smiled. Sister Linda had made it perfectly clear she wouldn't marry Mark and be stuck for life having to polish and clean all that junk his mama would make her take. No way. On her list Mark figured somewhat above the fine old pieces in her reasons for running from the machinations of the blue rinse cabal convened on Mama's wicker porch set and chomping on Miz Edna's delicacies. He was nowhere to be found on her dance card. Since she and Mark were pretty much friends, I figured she had her reasons, but as with anything else my "high-spirited" older sister decided, I also reckoned if she wanted me to know, she'd tell me.

I brought the bowl out to the porch, made the proper obeisance to old ladies, and was turning to go when Miz Santo grabbed my forearm with her liver-spotted claw.

"My, my, Miz Kramer, you certainly have a fine young man here. And the rabbi says…"

I shot a helpless, deer-in-the-headlights look at Mama. She knew I wasn't at all interested in what the rabbi had to say about me to the mate mongers. There were only three nice Jewish girls my age, and I knew full well they had picked out Tuna Fish Golden, so named for her uncanny resemblance to the erudite fish of the television commercials. I shuddered to think what bug he may have put in this old biddy's ear.

"Why, thank you, Miz Santo, we're proud of him," and smiling ever-so-maternally tender at me, "he's a good boy, a good student, and he's never given us a moment's trouble."

I smiled dutifully filial back at her, and her quick "freeze" look let me know that if I made mention of recently being under house restriction the sentence would be extended. To make my getaway, I gathered up the empty dishes to take inside, pausing long enough to catch the round of approval from the gathering on the porch.

"Now, Miz Kramer, about getting Mark and Linda together."

Mama faltered. She couldn't right her listing boat in time.

"Well…I…uh…"

Miz Santo pressed on.

"Mr. Santo and I are going to the get-together to welcome Mark home and we expect y'all to be there, now, you hear, and Miz Levy already said y'all were coming. We just need to make sure your Linda is coming, too."

I went upstairs to tell Linda she had just been sold down the river, and to get her parasol and crinoline ready.

"The hell you say! I hope y'all have a good time. I wouldn't take part in this charade if you paid me."

I sat on the edge of her bed, leafing through one of her travel books on Indonesia.

"Hey, don't blame me. I had nothing to do with it! That was all Lady Macbeth's doings and none of mine. But…"

I thought a second, trying to figure out how to phrase my question without jeopardizing the fragile truce Linda and I had established after her unceremonious early return from the state university.

"What's wrong with Mark?"

"Nothing. Nothing at all," she said turning to straighten the bottles on her dresser. "I'm just not in the market for a 'nice Jewish boy.' That's all. And if I were, Mark would be about the last one I'd pick."

"Why? I thought you liked him."

"I do."

"Then why…?"

"You know something, Little Brother? You may be smart in some things but you sure are dense in others. Come back in a couple of years, and we'll talk about it. How's Tuna Fish?"

"Whoa!" I laughed. "Step back!"

"Unh-hunh. Now you know how it feels."

"Well, anyway, we're off to the Levys come Sunday."

"You're off…your rocker!"

"All I gotta say is take that up with Mama."

"No need to. I'm leaving for New Orleans tonight. You can have the Levy fortune."

"Hunh?"

"Hey, get outta here. I've got shit to do."

Linda was as good as her word. She went to New Orleans on the back of a motorcycle with some James Dean lookalike hoodlum who was dressed in half the Argentine national production of leather. I helped Mama swallow her pride and went to have dinner with the Levys. It had all the promise of a script lifted straight from *The Graduate* but for the fact that our lead character was instead the antithesis of the angst-riddled Hoffmanesque interpretation.

Our not-Yeshiva-but-Yale guest of honor might as well have been King David himself for all his demeanor.

"God!" I thought. "What an arrogant ass!"

I hated him on sight. He stood for everything I was against in my full bloom of revolution sixties style. Everything about him was so obviously put together to create that odious enemy of the epoch, the bourgeois capitalist pig. His shoes would have withstood a military dress inspection. His hair—and this was the age of Aquarian *Hair*—was just ever-so-slightly longish, and he sported a Ringo Starr moustache. His suit was *tailored* even. I shuffled to meet him.

"Ah," he smiled ever-so-graciously extending the one hand for me to shake and the other open palm downward to clamp me heartily on the shoulder, all in one flawless movement. "Linda's little brother. And how are you?"

He smiled again, this time ever-so-wickedly with a wink to seal this manly bit of camaraderie. I was beginning to see why Linda didn't want to be tied to him.

"Nice to see you. Congratulations on your bourgeois credentials, Mr. Levy," I said.

"Ooh!" He smiled, side lip upturned. "We have a little Marxist here. So tell me, Comrade, what do you think of Stalin's minorities policies?"

"Well, since you asked, I think they sucked, and this has been one of the gravest criticisms brought against him. But I'm a Trotskyite, not a Stalinist."

I added the last with my own superior smirk.

"Ah, yes! And you can even speak the lingo. We must talk about this sometime."

He turned to Mama and Daddy.

"Bright boy. I assume this adolescent rebellion is not encouraged in the home."

"Fuck off!" I thought. "Come the revolution your kind of fascist pig will be nailed to the wall."

Mama sounded relieved, and smiled her best jasmine smile.

"I'm so glad to hear you say that, Mark. I wish you would talk to him. Don't you think that would be nice, Dear?"

My father mumbled to life.

"Yes, Honey, whatever you say."

Then turning to Mark, "Congratulations, Old Boy. I suppose now your daddy's going to be buying you a seat in the state legislature, won't he?"

Mark's father was beaming, slapping his scion on the back with a that's-my-boy thump which would have sent a less perfect masochist-with-no-self-respect tumbling into the guest line. But not Mark. No. This fellow was flawless. He even managed a grateful look to the benevolent patriarch, whose pride was thus increased.

I steamed all the way through dinner. Everything that asshole did seemed to point out some flaw in me. After dinner the bastard even big brothered me to the tennis court his bureaucrat parents had put in just for him. And of course there was the Jaguar in the garage, a gift from mère and père to Junior for some stellar achievement or another.

"Which had you rather do, Sport, play tennis or go swimming?"

Oh, yes. They had a pool, no doubt put in just for Mark to have pool parties and invite over the less fortunate. Oy!

"I'm not dressed for either."

"Not to worry. I'm sure there's a swim suit in the pool house somewhere," he said, sizing me up with a look of appraisal not unakin to Miz Santo which brought an involuntary smile to my face. "You should be able to wear some of my tennis clothes. Though, I'm not too sure about shoes. What size *do* you wear?"

I didn't miss the stress on "do," and he didn't miss that I didn't miss it, grinning just right to make it sound one step short of vulgar.

"Ten and a half, D."

"Well, imagine that," and he raised a foot. "Same size as me. Maybe we do have something in common after all."

I felt sick. Especially after Mr. Perfect showed his stuff on the court. What did I expect, anyway? And the worst part was that I had set out to whip his ass there, being not half-bad myself and good enough to have the tennis coach at school trying to get me signed up.

I shook his hand.

"Good match."

He smiled oh-so-charmingly gracious in victory.

"You'd play better if you got your hair cut out of your face, you know."

How dare he! My hair was my pride, shoulder length, thick, blond, and wavy. The teachers had to separate me from the Black girls who fought over the seats around me so they could play with it, calling me Goldilocks. I won't lie. It was a traffic stopper, and here comes some masculine Delilah.

"Fuck off!"

This time I said it out loud.

"Sit down."

He pointed to a low wall. I didn't move.

"Sit down, I said."

"Fuck off!"

"If I have to knock you down, I will."

He meant it.

"I will if you do. I'm not going to sit here while you try to lord yourself over me, you know."

He sat. I stiffly followed suit.

"Look, I know what you think. I'm just a bourgeois capitalist pig."

I said spitefully to his eyes, "Let's save the hail-fellow shit, shall we? I can't stand you, you pious, self-righteous, son-of-a-bitch, and I just want to get through this day without embarrassing my parents any more than Linda already has. Okay?"

He nodded his head in that gentlemanly attitude his breed have so mastered, sizing up their opponent.

"Okay. Let's go back in and be civil for the sake of empty social form, shall we?"

"What?" I spoke before thinking.

He smirked triumphantly.

"Nanh-anh, Little Brother. We don't want to be friends. Remember?"

He wore that triumphant smirk all the way back inside, wearing it as he winked at Mama.

"A hard case, I'm afraid, but smart and quick. Very quick."

I escaped to Mr. Levy's library and forgot my embarrassment among the volumes on the shelves. There were all matter of works in the original. Zola in French. Dante in Italian. Marx in German. Lenin in Russian. And titles and authors in the hundreds I did not recognize. I was looking at a row of ones familiar to me. I was pulling a volume from the shelf when I heard a voice behind me.

"Ah, Red Emma. One of my heroines. 'If I can't dance I want no part of your revolution.' That about sums up the way I feel about it, too. You know her?"

"Yes, I do."

I wasn't about to tell him I had a poster of her with that quote on my wall at home.

I flinched, instinctively drawing away from him.

"You know, Allen, you've truly misjudged me. You do know that, don't you?"

"Yeah. Tell you what, take me for a ride in your Jag out to the country club, let's do lunch, and talk about it."

"Okay, if that's what you want me to do, I will. I don't want you to dislike me without knowing who I am, okay?"

"Sure. Look, what did you study anyway at that ivory tower where you hid from the problems of the real world? Psychology?"

He smiled.

"Well, as a matter of fact, I did. Adolescent psychology to be exact. And I must say you're a case for the books."

"So you were hired by my mater and pater to reform me, right?"

"Oh, nothing quite so prosaic as all that. I have ulterior motives."

"Like what?"

"Like why don't I not tell you and just show you? You'd like that. The propaganda of the deed. But I'll just say for now that I find you interesting, and I'd like to get to know what makes you tick. That's all."

"Just lay off, okay? Take your Freudian perversions elsewhere."

"Astute, aren't we, Little Brother?"

"Fuck off. And quit calling me Little Brother."

"Hey, let's just try to be civil to begin with. Take this with you. Read it. Then we'll talk. You'll see…"

"Your father…"

"These books belong to me as much as they do to my father. I trust you with it. Just treat it with respect."

"I don't destroy books!" I fumed.

"I know. But sometimes you don't respect what's in them very much either."

He then left to rejoin the others, and I began to leaf through the book, looking for the comment on dancing.

CHAPTER 2

The next time I saw Mark was downtown at the Mimosa Café, paying his lunch tab and chatting with Nick the Greek. He saw me through the plate glass, pocketed his change, and came out to the street, calling my name. I winced as I saw him steady into perfect timing of his step to mine. When I paused, so did he in perfect synchronicity and with that infuriating two-armed movement from the Levy dinner party.

"Well, my little red friend, have you read the book yet?"

"I wish you wouldn't do that."

"Do what?"

He seemed genuinely puzzled.

"Pat me on the shoulder and shake hands whenever we meet."

"Oh, sorry." He stepped back and in flourishing sincerity raised his arm, fist clinched. "Greetings comrade! Power to the working classes, and death to the capitalist oppressors! Is that more like it?"

"Oh, fuck off."

I turned to go.

He smiled, matching his step to mine.

"So, that's the best you can come up with? 'Fuck off?' Surely you can be more original and less vulgar."

"Oh, excuse me, Mr. Levy," I stopped and turned to face him. "I did not mean to offend your refined sensibilities. Just what the hell do you want from me?"

"Your mind."

He was serious.

"I thought I had already laid yours and Mama's plans for my psychological readjustment to rest. Go play missionary elsewhere, Pope Sigmund. I don't need it, I don't want it, and I'll fight y'all every step of the way."

"Oh, I know you will. That's what makes you so interesting."

I turned again to go.

"Where are you off to in such a hurry?"

"I've got something to do."

"Ah, that's too bad. Have you had lunch?"

"Say what?"

"Have you had lunch?" He did that pause thing between each word, like he was talking to a retard.

"Yes."

"Well, I guess that cancels that out then."

"Cancels what out?"

"Inviting you to have lunch at the club so you can spend some time getting to know the bourgeois Mr. Levy in his natural environment."

"You just got through with lunch."

"Ah, but I would gladly have another just to spend the afternoon with you."

"I believe you would. Why?"

"I'm bored?"

He was grinning.

"You make me sick. I ought to go with you just to embarrass you in there where you think you're one of 'em. Never mind what kind of Jew boy they're calling you behind your back. Never mind your grandfather would not have been allowed through the front door. I despise you fucking court Jews."

He stopped cold. His arm reached out to halt me.

"You just hold on there, mister. First off, my great-grandfather was a charter member of that club. Got it? Okay, so we may be court Jews. I'm not ashamed of that. Why don't we talk about that? Just because you don't like me is no reason to impinge… And where did you get that term, anyway?"

"Hannah Arendt."

He looked at me with a change of expression, sort of one of quizzical admiration.

"Indeed? What have you read of hers?"

I rattled off several of the titles.

"Okay, you may not be so illiterate after all. And?"

"And what?"

"Do you agree or disagree with her thesis?"

"Which thesis?"

"The one you're charging me with."

"Which is?"

"That court Jews have traditionally been the primary agents in bringing communal destruction on the Jewish masses."

I unfroze a bit.

"Yeah. That's it."

"Would you like to discuss that?"

I did, but I wouldn't.

"No. I don't like you."

He laughed, sticking his tongue out, waving his fingers with his thumbs hooked in his ears.

"Well, I don't care. Nyanh-nyanh. Look, can't we just try to understand each other?"

"Why? What do I stand to gain from that?"

"An education."

"Are you trying to imply something?"

"Yes. You need some heavy duty training before you get yourself into trouble. You can't go around calling people fascist pigs. It's not very smart. Just smart mouthed."

"You *are* a fascist pig."

"Oink, oink. No doubt, but you don't know me. You just know what you think you've seen. How old are you?"

"Fifteen."

"Ohhh! Almost grown, aren't you? Right. 'Fuck off.' C'mon. Let's drop politics. What would you like to do?"

"Plant trees on a kibbutz in Israel, scale the Great Wall of China...I don't know. Anything but talk to you."

Mark looked curious.

"You know I've liked you ever since I first took notice of you when you were rubbing Myra Franklin's face in dog shit."

I laughed, feeling somewhat more at ease.

"You remember that? We couldn't have been more than five or six when that happened."

"You and Myra weren't, but I was. I was proud of you."

"Mama gave me a whipping. And Daddy and Miz Edna did, too. "

"I know. I thought that wasn't fair, and I told them so. She had it coming."

She did, I thought. I had never repented of that bit of ungentlemanly behavior against the Methodist minister's snotty daughter. She knew I couldn't hit a girl, so she waited on me in ambush, practicing a mean left hook and half nelson. One day I just had enough and struck back.

I felt myself warm a little toward Mark, reassessing my view of his offer of friendship. And he *was* smart. Maybe he was right. Maybe he could teach me something. I smiled.

"Linda bought me a milkshake!"

"So, wanna go for a swim?"

"I'll have to think about it. But just not at the country club. I'd rather die."

"Okay. I'll get in touch. Swimming. Somewhere besides the country club. Right?"

"Maybe."

"Okay. Maybe. I'll settle for that. I'll call you. Tell your folks and Linda I said 'hi.'"

And he was off. There are those words that describe something, but you never actually hear anybody say them, right? Well he *sauntered* off, lightly whistling what I suppose was his victory hymn, going the opposite direction to which we had been walking.

I delivered his messages at home. Linda cornered me in the back yard where I lay on the hammock rereading Mark's book.

"What you reading?"

I showed her the cover.

"Don't you think you may be carrying this shit a little far, Chairman Mao?"

"You don't understand. The true liberation..."

"Oh, shut up! You sound like a bad record with that crap. Where do you find that stuff anyway?"

"Here and there." Then I added smugly, "I got this one Sunday from your intended."

"He's not my intended, and I'm not sure I like his influence on you very much."

To my surprise, I found myself rushing to his defense.

"He doesn't believe *all* of this..."

I caught myself before I went to telling her about the revolution and dancing.

"Besides, he's a fascist just like his daddy and the rest of their bourgeois..."

She laughed.

14

"Well, no need to worry. I just wish you still read things like *The Call of the Wild*."

"I do. Jack London was a leftist. His books…"

She broke in in a sing-song, "…are still popular in the Soviet Union."

She returned to her normal voice.

"I've been to school, too, you know. And I think it was me who told you that in the first place. Now, let me get out of here before I'm subjected to another one of your interminably boring diatribes. I'm going to have to have a talk with Mark about you."

"Why not? Let's just go ahead and make it a family project my psychological maladjustment, shall we?"

Linda went back inside where I could see her through the window, talking, arguing might be a better word, with Mama. I heard the phone ring as I went back to my book. After a paragraph or two, Mama's call to the phone interrupted me. She brought it outside to the patio chairs, left it, and went back inside to pick up her discussion with Linda. Their voices were audible, if unintelligible, from where I sat and picked up the phone. I was surprised to hear Mark's voice.

"So? How's about it? Wanna go to the beach this weekend?"

"I told you…"

"You said maybe. And it's camping. Roughing it real proletarian style. I promised you no country clubs. How about it?"

"Let me talk to my parents."

"I already talked to your mom. She said she thought it would be fine. She said she'd clear it with your dad and get back with me. So? Wanna give it a shot?"

"Who else is going?"

"Just the two of us."

"To get me alone, no escape, for the big brother talk. Right?"

15

"Something like that. But really just to have some fun."

"Are you sure you can take it. I mean such primitive conditions for your refined…"

"Hey, three days with no politics, okay? I told you, we'll have fun. I like sleeping on the beach under the stars."

"You can't sleep on the beach. It's against the law."

"Not if you know where to go."

"Oh, I see. A beach club that will let you sleep on the beach. That is, unless you're a bum. I'd just as soon not."

"Oh, come off it. I know a place where even *your* sensitivities, however put on, won't be offended. I swear, I think your mother must have been scared by McCarthy when she was carrying you. I'll call later to see what your dad had to say."

I hung up, and was opening the kitchen door just in time to hear Linda.

"Mama! Open your eyes, would you! How can you possibly…"

She broke off, but Mama, with her back to me, continued.

"Linda, I don't see what you've got against the Levy Boy. He's nice, he's got a good education, he's from a good family, and he's been so sweet to take up time with Allen now just when…"

I laughed, startling Mama to silence, and I picked up her thought, winking at my sister and mimicking Mama's "concerned" voice.

"…your little brother is getting out of hand with all that stuff he's been reading."

I paused.

"Worry not, Sister Mine. I'll not let him get his foot through your door by playing big brother to me."

Linda left the room, rolling her eyes heavenward. Mama turned to me.

"Go help Edna on the side porch. Miz Santo's coming over in a little while, and I'll not have her telling everybody what a sloppy house I keep."

"Yes, ma'am."

"What did you tell Mark?"

"I…"

She cut me off.

"I'm so glad you're hitting it off so well. I worry so much about you what with your daddy so tied up with his work, and you," she rubbed the fuzz on my upper lip, "growing up right before my very eyes into a young man."

"Mah-muh!"

I winced away and went to help Miz Edna. I was going to the beach for the weekend for sure now. I made a silent vow to go through Mama's reading and burn her psychology books.

CHAPTER 3

Early Friday morning Mark was, as promised, loading me up before dawn for the two-hour drive to the Coast. I was putting the rod and reel into the back of a truck marked as belonging to some department of the state government.

"So, we're going at the taxpayers' expense. No doubt due to Papa's courteous foresight?"

He put his finger to his lips

"Sssh. No politics. We promised. You like fishing?"

"No."

"Then why are you bringing a rod, reel, and tackle box?"

"To make Daddy happy."

"Okay. In that case we'll just have to stop at a fish market on the way back."

He skillfully and effortlessly secured the tarp, also marked state property, over the back. I was pissed. Even in blue jeans and a ball cap, he was perfect. He smiled a flash of perfect white teeth as if on cue to my thoughts.

"Ready, Freddy?"

He walked over to where I stood watching.

"You slap me on the back, motherfucker, and I'll…"

"Hey, cool down, would you? We've got three whole days for this. Okay?"

Mama came down the drive with a thermos and paper bag in hand.

"I fixed you boys some coffee and had Edna make you rolls. Y'all be good. Drive carefully, and take good care of my baby boy."

"Mah-muh!"

"Mah-muh, nothing. You are my baby. Now make sure to use this suntan lotion when you're on the beach, and…"

"Mama, I'm a big boy. I can take care of myself."

Mark smiled that disgusting flash of teeth.

"I'll take good care of him, Miz Kramer."

Mama hugged me again.

"Now you behave and do just what Mark tells you. Y'all have a good time. We'll see you Sunday evening?"

I rolled my eyes upward just in time to catch a shadowy movement behind Linda's darkened window.

We got in, and he drove off, Mark, of course, perfectly obeying even the minutest traffic rules on the deserted streets of town as we headed for the freeway.

"Pour me some coffee, would you?"

I obliged, and silently passed him the steaming thermos cup. He sipped on the hot liquid, blowing to cool it as the lights of town faded behind us.

"Smoke?" He asked.

"Cigarettes?"

"No. Marijuana."

"No," I lied.

"Too bad," he said fishing a, you got it, perfectly rolled joint from his shirt pocket. "I do. Hope you don't mind."

Mind? I wished I hadn't been so quick. A good high would make this a lot easier, and getting high was no easy task for kids my age in those days.

Holding a lungful, he passed the joint to me.

"Here. Cut the bullshit. We're supposed to be going to have a good time. Remember?"

I took it.

"Good to see you're not above a few decadent habits of the bourgeoisie."

"I hardly…" I spluttered, coughing up the smoke, "think that smoking a little dope is a bourgeois pastime. Now scotch…"

"And," he said with that sarcastic tone that I knew by now meant I was about to get one of his dressings-down for which I'd have no retort. "Before we lay this aside, tell me my young internationalist, just how much do you think your average Mexican pot-growing peon makes per pound of this stuff? This, my friend, is the height of capitalist running dog imperialism in the third world."

He inhaled and passed the joint back to me.

"Clip it, will you? There's a roach clip in that bag of shit on the seat."

I followed his orders, properly executing the clipping mechanics.

"I see you've done this before my non-smoking compadre. But you're right. Never admit it. "

He paused.

"Tell me something, why do you hate me the way you do?"

"Because you're a pig."

"Oink-oink back at you. We've covered that, and rather exhaustively I might add. No, it's something else. But if you don't want to talk about it, that's okay by me."

The smoke was beginning to take effect. Mark drove on in silence, eyes straight ahead. He really wasn't such a bad sort, I thought. A little too…

I spoke up.

"You really want to know?"

"Yeah. Really."

I found myself answering, the usual tone of belligerence softened considerably which caught him and me both off guard.

"You're so goddamn perfect. Not a blemish anywhere."

I looked down at his feet.

"Look at you fucking shoestrings. All four bows are the same size. The ends are the same length. You gripe my ass."

"Perfect?"

"Yes, you're perfect. You're a sanctimonious asshole, and a perfect one of those, too."

"Nope. Not perfect. Just comfortable and self-assured. But," his voice took on a distanced tone, "I'm not immune to human frailties. I wake up in the middle of the night scared of demons under the bed, too. Do you know what I'm scared of?"

"A stock market crash?"

"No. I'm scared I'll be alone. I mean without having someone to love. Someone to love me...for what I am..."

"You? Ha! Worry not! The yentas have seen to that already."

"I'm afraid I'm no more interested in your sister than she is in me. That's a match made on your mama's side porch, not in heaven."

"What's wrong with my sister?"

He flashed his teeth.

"Absolutely nothing. Put down the dueling pistols. I like your sister very much. She's a sweet kid and will be a catch for some lucky fellow. But she's not for me or me for her."

"Ah, yes. Wrong class. We wouldn't want the fabulous Levy fortune to wind up in the wrong hands, would we?"

"Hey. None of that. If I told you my name was Higgenbotham and I drove a semi, would you think better of me?"

"Hardly."

I laughed.

"I can just see you..."

"Driving a semi? FYI, I do know how."

"Come off it! You wouldn't know..."

"Oh, yes, I would. My Uncle Robert put me to work on the loading docks one summer when I was about your age. One of the drivers took me under wing and taught me how. He said I was not a bad student and had possibilities. I guess you could say I was perfect there, too, eh?"

"Oh, yes. Slumming with the coolies, no doubt."

"Something like that. Call it what you will, but I do know the basics of handling a semi. Now all I've got to do is convince you that my name is Higgenbotham, and we might get to be friends after all."

I muttered something unintelligible. We rode on in silence with me watching the sunrise on the horizon.

Mark broke the silence.

"So, how's Charlie?"

"Who?"

"Tuna Fish Golden. How is she?"

"How would I know? I hardly ever see her except at temple."

"Y'all don't go to school together?"

"Yeah. But we run in different crowds. She's too straight."

"Straight?"

"Yeah. Like you. Miss Goody Two Shoes. With buck teeth."

"You play football?"

"No."

"Basketball?"

"No."

"Anything?"

"No."

I decided not to tell him about the tennis coach.

"What *do* you do?"

"Read."

"I already knew that. Did you read Red Emma yet?"

"Nope."

I lied. I had, but I wasn't going to tell him I had.

"Okay." He paused. "You should."

"I don't think you need to tell me what I should and should not do. Okay?"

"Hey! Don't let me stop your stupidity. But I beg to differ. You do. This phase of yours won't last long in the real world."

I shut up. In the silence I watched as the shapes of the pines along the roadway became distinct, and listened to the faraway sounds of the countryside coming to life merging with the thump-thump of tires on asphalt.

"You want to know something, Allen?"

"What?"

"You're right."

"About what?"

"About the Levys being court Jews."

He tapped the wheel with his open palm, glanced to gauge my level of attention, and spoke.

"You know my great-great-grandfather?"

"The colonel? I don't think we ever met."

"Smart ass. Do you know what happened to his parents?"

"No."

"They were deported."

"From Russia?"

"No. From Tennessee."

"When? For what?"

"For being court Jews. No other reason."

"Say what?"

"December, 1862. Arrested, loaded up, and sent packing under guard with only what they could carry with them."

"I thought your great-great-grandfather was a colonel."

"He was."

"And they still deported his folks?"

"Not the Confederates. The Yankees."

"For real?"

"For real. It's in the records."

"And? So what?"

"Well, they were court Jews and when the crown changed hands, they went packing."

"And what does that mean?"

"It means that being a court Jew isn't all it's cracked up to be. Do you think I like the role I'm in? Do you think I like playing all these silly games, floating about in 'society,' preening, and being ten times what I have to be to prove something? To be...I don't know...some kind of exceptional image. Do you think I *liked* growing up under that portrait's stare, knowing every time I saw the sabre slash that it didn't matter how good I was at it, it could be gone in a flash? Always having to look good, do the right thing, all because I was a Levy. I wish to God I were Homer Higgenbotham and not Mark Levy."

I looked into his face. Something serious and bitter had taken hold of his features, had remolded, resculpted, altered, changed his appearance in a metamorphosis before my very eyes. It was almost as if he were mesmerized by some hideous image only he could see.

"Hey, don't be so hard on yourself. There's worse things to be than a Levy, you know."

"Being a Levy is no problem. It's handed you on a silver platter, fed you with the proverbial silver spoon. It's being Mark Levy that's the problem. I don't know why I even came back..."

His gaze drifted into the still distance along with his voice.

I felt a strange closeness to the man driving. I began to think about myself and the way I had treated him. After all, I, too, had read only his Levy nameplate, and had not bothered to distinguish Mark from Levy.

"I'm sorry," I said.

"For what?"

"For treating you like a shit. I guess all that would weigh you down. But, well, hey, you do buy into it, you know."

"And why shouldn't I? Sackcloth and ashes won't change the fact I've been brought up in it. It's my place. My fate, I suppose. I just want to find a space, a little tiny corner, somewhere just to be me."

"You will. You just have to keep looking."

He reached over, tousled my hair, and smiled as always all toothy, but with what I realized perhaps for the first time, was just a touch of sadness. But quickly his voice lost its dark tenor and his dark eyes took on a light and welcome twinkle.

"Look at who's counseling whom!"

So, I thought. It *was* a set-up between him and Mama all along. And I had almost been taken in by it. I sullenly returned to my corner, angry at myself for having been foolish enough to fall for such shabby trickery. I feigned sleep.

I don't know what I was expecting from the camping trip. Whatever it was, it didn't come about. The time, as I recall it now, passed in a vague haze. Mark's "spot" was secluded and quiet. There was a small white sand beach beneath a mini cliff with a pathway worn from years of not-so-secret use. Remains of a few campfires dotted black on the sand, and as soon as the tent was pitched in his Eagle Scout manner, Mark policed the area collecting past campers' beer cans, bottles, and other non-biodegradable trash. Two days of conversation produced no memorable friction. Books, movies, records, and other such popular topics filled the time between long silences.

I found myself by the time we were packing up really beginning to wish the time was not over. We had been lying on the beach in the sun. As we moved about taking the camping gear up the hill to the state vehicle, there was a change in the air. The quiet solitude was now charged with an intense electricity. The few words Mark spoke were strained and nearly strangled.

As we were tying down the tarp, Mark was suddenly chipper. "One more dip before we go?"

"Sure," I said, pulling my tee shirt over my head. "Why not?"

Mark followed my action and at the foot of the path he challenged me to a race to the buoy floating several yards into the water. On count, we plunged in and in a few strokes, I was easily outdistanced. Gamely plugging on, I returned to the shore as he was toweling off. He stopped in mid-motion, the towel on his still wet hair, as I stepped out of the water and onto the sand. He stood that way several moments, looking straight toward me. Instinctively, I looked down at my form, searching for clinging seaweed or some such. There was nothing.

Mark must have noticed. He jerked slightly, blinking his eyes several times.

"You're burnt! You didn't wear the suntan lotion your mom packed."

The tingling prickling of my skin as I shivered in the warming sun verified his observation. Turning to check his condition, I was not surprised to find he was only more deeply tanned. I had not yet noticed the unclothed Mark, not really. His body was as flawless as the rest of him. Not overdone, just healthily defined and tight with just the lightest trail of black leading from his navel to the waist of his cutoff jeans. He looked, I thought, the picture of the all-American boy, and for the first time since the drive down, I felt the anger rising again. Grabbing my own towel I began to dry off as I headed back up the trail.

That still picture of Mark standing and staring stayed in my mind throughout the mostly silent ride home, and later that night as I was going through the ritual pre-sleep masturbation, the image persisted. I was not a virgin. I liked girls. I knew which ones "did" and which ones "didn't," and courted the former. But now, instead of full breasts and rounded hips, my fantasies kept coming to that one stark moment of Mark on the beach.

I pulled up my pajama bottoms, turned on the bedside lamp, and reached for the book on the nightstand. I read a few lines but the words jumbled and danced in front of my eyes, mixed in with the image of Mark. I put on a robe and went downstairs to heat some milk and make chocolate. As I walked through the den. I glanced at Daddy's liquor cabinet. Quietly, I poured into a glass what I knew was probably too much to pass the Old Man's calculating eye. I went out onto the patio. I was shuddering from the burning in my gullet when I heard the screen door. I jumped around to see Linda.

"Little Brother, you shouldn't be doing that."

"Don't tell Daddy," I said automatically in the special tone known to all sibling partners in perfidy.

"I won't, but you shouldn't be doing that. Especially this time at night and alone on the patio."

"The folks are asleep."

"That's still not what I mean. What's wrong?"

The unexpected tenderness with which Linda flicked a strand of hair out of my face opened something inside of me and in a rush of uncontrolled relief, I started to cry. Without a word Linda took me in her arms and patted me while I sobbed.

"Linda," I said at last, "I need to talk to somebody. I need to ask you something. Please, please promise me you won't say anything to anybody."

"I won't," she said, breaking the embrace, but continuing to stroke my hair. "I promise. What is it?"

"I don't know…I mean…" Then I blurted out, "Am I queer?"

She jerked back her hand, her face dark with anger.

"What did that motherfucker do to you?"

All of the sudden I knew why she and Mark wouldn't, couldn't, play the game with Miz Santo and Miz Feinstein. Unable to stop myself, I began to cry again.

"Nothing."

She grabbed my shoulders.

"Tell me the truth!"

The unexpected tone frightened me.

"Tell me! If he laid a hand on you, I'll kill him! How could Mama and Daddy be so fucking, goddamn stupid letting you go off alone with him...I..."

It was my turn to be comforting.

"Linda, I promise you nothing happened. Nothing. Is Mark queer?"

"Yes. Yes, he is."

She paused.

"Fuck! Fuck it! Goddamn him! I told him..."

"You told him what?"

She spat out.

"To keep his fucking hands off of you!" Her voice raised. "I'll kill him!"

"Sssh! Not so loud! You'll wake the neighbors up."

"I'll do more than that!"

I could see the famous Linda temper coming to a boil, and while I didn't know what "more than that" might entail, I wasn't willing to risk it to find out.

"Linda, I told you. He didn't touch me. Nothing like that."

She calmed perceptively.

"Then why do you want to know if you're queer?"

I was trying to find the right words.

"I...I just...I mean I've been having these thoughts...I mean...well, not about girls...you know?"

Linda sat quietly a moment, moved, then spoke calmly, too calmly, in measured cadence.

"Have you ever slept with a girl?"

I answered, teenage male pride rising.

"Yes. Plenty. I'm not a virgin!"

"Okay. Don't get all upset. Did…do…you like it?"

"Yes."

"Well, then, why worry? Go get laid. You're not queer. Just confused. Okay?"

"I guess."

"Stay away from Mark."

I spoke without realizing what I was saying.

"I don't know if I want to."

Linda froze.

"Okay. But if I were you, I think I'd be a little more sure."

"Linda," I waited a second to be certain I had her attention. "Don't say anything to Mark. Okay?"

CHAPTER 4

Linda meant business when she said she was out to get as far away as possible. She left "to travel." She only said she was going to Indonesia, Malaysia, India, and Nepal. She left no itinerary as to when she would be where and how long she'd stay. She sent the de rigueur picture postcards, an occasional letter to Mama and Daddy, and longer more activities detailed ones to me which she signed. "Your big sister, Sarah Dippity, and glad you're not here."

Her leaving had thwarted the machinations of the marriage brokers, the porch gatherings taking on a new intensity in the days preceding her departure. She had never again mentioned our conversation on the patio. Perhaps it was only my imagination, but she had seemed to be watching me as if I were some strange new bacterium isolated under the microscope. I conscientiously had begun to plan my day to avoid being around her.

Even after she left, I spent the long days riding my bicycle to the river and lying on the tree-covered bluffs, reading, and thinking. I kept a close watch on my body for any physical changes, outward signs of metamorphosis.

I was putting my bike up when Daddy came into the garage.

"Hey, Son. I've been looking for you all afternoon. Where've you been?"

"Down at the river."

"Fishing?"

"No, sir."

His eyebrows raised in his own peculiar manner, a motion I knew meant he wanted a better answer.

Spinning the combination lock on the chain, I added, "Just reading and thinking."

I remembered the still unused rod and reel he'd bought for my camping trip with Mark. I lied.

"Benji Johnson and I want to go up river one day if we can, though. He saw the rod and reel you bought me and he got his daddy to get him one like it, and..."

I checked myself before I got into it any deeper.

"Well, that may have to wait a while," he said. "I wanted to talk to you about something. You're getting big enough now to be trusted alone. I want to do something special for your mama on our anniversary."

The special day was coming up, and I had forgotten. Twenty years, August the third. I had to think of a present.

"Yessir?"

"I want to take her back to Copenhagen."

He was smiling broadly, obviously pleased with himself. Mama had spent a year in Denmark as an exchange student after the war. She met Daddy there. He was with the occupation forces in Germany and had gone to Copenhagen, as he said, to get rid of the bad taste in his mouth. Armed with a letter-of-introduction from Great-Aunt Mildred, he called on Mama, and a storybook romance resulted.

I smiled back.

"That's great! When are y'all leaving?"

"In a rush or something, Son? Got something lined up already? Who is she?"

I reddened as I always did whenever Daddy wanted to talk about girls. I mumbled something.

"Well, you keep it down and don't let your mama get wind of it, especially from any of the neighbors. No wild parties. Next Friday." He continued, "Edna'll be here as usual. Don't make it any worse for her than it already is. Your Uncle Henry'll be checking on you every once in a while." He gave me a fatherly punch-on-the-arm. "But, you'll make out."

Mama was all in a dither. For the next few days a steady stream of well-wishers paraded in and out between shopping trips with my two aunts. On Thursday, we went to see Great-Aunt Mildred at the nursing home and took her out to dinner. Mama and Daddy were her favorites, and the childless old lady had always had a special place in her heart for Linda and me. Her presents to us were always special and a little nicer than those she gave the other grandnieces and nephews.

The old lady was beaming, satisfied.

"You know, Allen, I introduced your mama and daddy."

"Yes, ma'am."

I knew. And in case I ever forgot, she told me the story ever chance she got. But this time instead of going into the story again, she looked away and turned to Mama.

"Miz Ruth Golden came to call the other day." She shifted her gaze this time to Daddy before continuing. "She brought Roberta's little girl with her. She's certainly turning into a fine young lady."

"Yes, ma'am," I said hoping to alter the course the conversation had taken. "If you like Tuna Fish."

Coffee cups stopped in mid sip, and, realizing the error too late, I added.

"She looks like Charlie Tuna on the commercial."

Sips resumed, and so did Great-Aunt Mildred's prattle.

"I grant you that. But she's a nice girl, and comes from a good family. Ruth and I were schoolmates back in The Age of Pericles, you know, and…"

I knew this, too. So did Tuna Fish. She did a great impression of her granny's half-senile ramblings about the mischief these two old birds had gotten into, the night they had dressed as ghosts and were caught "haunting" the cemetery, or the time they "borrowed" Miz Ruth's daddy's Model T, or the time…

The reminiscing lulled me into a false sense of security, and I was thinking of something else entirely when I heard her saying, "We'll just have to do something to bring them together."

The horror must have registered perceptibly on my face.

Daddy glanced knowingly at me before he spoke.

"Well, Miz Mildred, that may be a little premature. Allen's playing the field right now. Right, Son?"

"Oh, yessir," I said, thankful for a change for his attention. "That's right, I…"

Mama's sharp toe under the table put an end to the rest.

"Anyway, Son," the old woman said. "I just want you to be happy. And good. I've got something for you to celebrate your new responsibility."

She fumbled through the tissues, handkerchiefs, and assorted other detritus of the old lady's magpie nest in her ancient handbag. She at length presented me with an envelope with my name scrawled across the front in her Victorian script.

"Thank you, ma'am," I said, rising in my chair to lean over and peck her on her wrinkled cheek, my nose crinkling at the smell which seemed the special odor of elderly females.

I laid the envelope aside.

"Aren't you going to open it?"

I felt embarrassed, but followed her order. The amount was staggering. More than she had sent Linda off with on her trip.

"Aunt Mildred…," I stammered.

She shushed me, winking conspiratorially.

"Hush up! This is yours to do with whatever you want, and I don't want your mama and daddy watching to see either. It's my gift to you and has nothing to do with them."

As she spoke, she handed another envelope to my parents.

"Besides, I've got something for them. Happy anniversary, children."

In the profuse "oh-Aunt-Mildred-you-shouldn't-haves" which followed, I wondered about the gift. It was twice what she had given me for my bar mitzvah. I silently hoped that my parents would respect her wishes. If they knew the amount, they'd surely make me do something "sensible" with it.

I got my wish. In the rush of last-minute details, Great-Aunt Mildred's check was forgotten, and the next day I took off downtown to cash it and buy my parents an anniversary present. Mission accomplished, I returned home to help them finish packing. Uncle Henry came to take them to the airport. On the freeway back into town, he began trying to get me to at least spend the night at their place.

"Nossir, thank you, though. I'm sort of looking forward to being alone."

"Well, Boy, you've got a month of it. Edith's cooking her pot roast…"

He trailed off in a laugh, and I joined in. Aunt Edith's pot roast was infamous. She was a good cook, but pot roast wasn't her specialty even if it was "special."

I liked Uncle Henry. He was Daddy's younger brother. He and Aunt Edith had three daughters, but no sons. Even though Uncle Henry had been a star athlete in college, still played mean tennis, and regularly ran marathons, he never macho'ed me, disparagingly referring to Daddy's inclinations that direction as "Hebrew Tarzanism."

As we turned onto our street, Uncle Henry offered the spare room once again. Again I refused.

"Oh, all right," he said. "Look, Son, have a good time."

He turned somewhat serious, but his eyes still crinkling.

"Be safe and don't let your parents down."

"I will. And I won't. Thanks for the ride. I'll call y'all."

"Good. Want to come over for dinner on Sunday?"

"Sure. Thanks. No pot roast, though. Okay?"

"Okay. I'll tell Edith."

"Don't you dare!"

He saluted as I got out and headed up the back walk.

The house was eerily quiet. Miz Edna had left enough food for me to feed six along with detailed instructions on what to do to "heat it up, and eat it up." I passed over the dishes, grabbed a cola from the 'fridge, went straight to the liquor cabinet, fixed a drink, and full of manhood, started calling up my friends to brag about my new state of freedom. Leafing through my address book, a gift from Uncle Henry complete with a "rating" system of stars, Mark's name caught my attention.

I sat several minutes before dialing. His mother answered.

"I'm sorry. He's out of town. May I ask who's calling, please?"

I told her.

"Oh, hey, Sugar. Did your folks get off okay?"

"Yes, ma'am."

"I'm so happy for them…" And she rambled off chattering about how much she and Mr. Levy liked Copenhagen, how nice the Danes were, Mark's first visit to Tivoli, and God knows what all else.

Finally, she asked, "What did you need for me to tell him?"

"Ma'am?"

Josef Nix

"Mark. What did you want me to tell him?"

"Oh, uh…" I tried to think of a message. "I've finished with a book he loaned me, and I wanted to bring it back."

"Well, Hon, he won't be back until the middle of the week, if…"

"If it's okay, I can drop it by tomorrow when I'm out that way."

"Isn't that kind of far?"

"No, ma'am. I'm riding my bike out to the river. I'll drop it by. That is, if someone is going to be at home."

"I'm going to be out, but Mr. Levy'll be here at least the first part of the day. But if you want, now, I'll just tell Mark. I mean, don't make a special trip just to drop it off."

"No, ma'am. It's no trouble. I'll drop it by."

"Okay, I'll tell Mr. Levy to expect you. If he's not here, just put it between the screen and wood doors. We'll look for it. So, how've you been enjoying independence?"

"Fine," I mumbled, thinking to myself that I'd know a lot better if I could get off the phone and get to it. We said our goodbyes, and I hung up.

Mark's image on the beach followed me about the house, flickering on the television set, looking at me with that strange, still gaze from the Ricardos' living room, replacing the programmed antics of Lucy and Ethel. It surfaced from the pages of *Life* magazine, and rendered incomprehensible Steinbeck's words.

I went for a long walk, ambling about the quiet neighborhood streets where I knew everyone, and where I had a security of belonging to something beyond myself. My earlier restlessness began to ease.

The next morning, I rang the bell at the Levy house, hoping that Mr. Levy would not answer. No such luck. I almost laughed aloud as I saw him looking through the glass. He was dressed in his idea of "at home casual," Bermuda shorts, polo shirt, flip-flops, and his famous cigar clamped at the side of his mouth.

"Well, well. It's the Kramer orphan. Come in. Come in."

I recalled Mark's comments about his father's habit of repeating everything.

"Thank you, sir, but I really don't have time. I just wanted to make sure I got this back to Mark."

I held out the book.

"Please tell Mark thank you."

I wanted to beat a hasty retreat before Mr. Levy passed comment on the book.

"So, Red Emma. Red Emma. A most interesting person, she was. Most interesting and most misunderstood. Most misunderstood. This book belonged to my father. The old codger made me read it. Said I needed to understand the dangers of anarchism. It was a big thing back then. You know anarchists are still barred from immigration? Them, homosexuals, and lunatics. Somewhat redundant, hunh?"

"Yessir," I mumbled. "I really am sorry to be in such a rush, but I'm meeting someone, and…"

"Making hay while the sun shines, eh? Go for it, son. Go for it. Enjoy yourself while you still can. I'll let Junior know you stopped by."

"Please do," I said, I thought maybe a bit too effusively, and took my leave.

CHAPTER 5

Early Wednesday morning, I awoke to Miz Edna's calling me to the phone.

"Got it!" I yelled reaching for the receiver on the nightstand, and rubbing the sleep from my eyes, I answered, listening for the click from Miz Edna's end.

"Good morning! Rise and shine and let's go fishing!"

"Who...?"

"How soon they forget. This is Mark."

"What do you want?"

"Hey! Is that the way to talk to somebody calling to take you fishing?"

"You already know I don't like fishing."

"Right. Okay, then, am I invited to your party?"

"What party?"

"The one you're having while your parents are gone."

"I hadn't planned..."

"Oh, my! You *are* a stick in the mud. Don't you know you have to or they won't think you're normal?"

The image flashed before my eyes, flickered a moment, danced, and became clearer.

"Mark?"

"Yes? What?"

"Mark...I'd like to see you."

It was his turn to be silent.

"Okay?"

"Sure," he said. "When? Why?"

I answered only his first question.

"Tonight."

"Sure. Are you all right?"

"Of course. Why not?"

"You just sound a little odd. That's all. Look, I'm free this afternoon. Why don't I come over around lunchtime and we can go see the tamale man, get some tamales, and go out to the lake."

"Sounds good, but Miz Edna's already laid down the law. She's pissed off at me for not eating her food. She's ordered me to eat here today."

"Okay. So what's she fixing?"

"Soup."

"Is it good?"

"The best! She went to see her folks in the country and came back loaded with all kinds of shit from their garden. She says she'll just have to put all my vegetables into a single pot to get me to eat right!"

"Think she'll mind another mouth to feed?"

"I'll see." I yelled down the stairs. "Miz Edna! Is it all right if I invite somebody for lunch?"

"Yeah," she yelled back. "If they'll eat."

"Fine," I said back into the telephone. "About noon?"

Date completed, I hung up the phone and was stretching back out onto the bed when Miz Edna rapped at the door.

"You going to lay around in bed all day? I got work to do around here. You ain't changed them bedclothes since before your mama left."

It was true. Obviously, Mama had said something to her before leaving. Miz Edna usually respected mine and Linda's privacy, never bothering our rooms except under Mama's express orders.

"You going to get up or lay around all day?"

"I'm going to lay around all day."

"Not with me in this house, you ain't. You 'spect me to serve you *and* your company in bed? Get up! Who's coming to eat?"

"Mark."

"Who?"

"Mark. Mark Levy."

Miz Edna's head popped through the door, her face registering quizzical surprise.

"Who?"

"Mark Levy. A friend of mine."

She stood in the doorway, her gaze fixed and her face immobile. Her speech was measured.

"A friend of yours? He belong to the Levys stay out there off Riverside?"

"Yes, ma'am."

"And your mama and daddy know 'bout this?"

"About me inviting him to lunch?"

Miz Edna's eyes flashed.

"Nossir. 'Bout you traipsing around with a grown man while they gone. I don't like this at all."

"They know he's my friend."

"And your mama think it's all right?"

"Yes, ma'am."

I was getting unnerved by this Torquemada in Moorish mufti.

"You better get used to having him around. He's Linda's intended."

"Hmmmph!"

She started to yanking dirty laundry from the piles I had let grow while Mama was readying for the trip.

"Somebody better tell *her* about it. She don't act like she's got no beau to me, traipsing about the other side of the world with a bunch of folks that think they granmaw's a cow. Don't you never wash no clothes? These tennis shoes smells like a sewage plant."

Miz Edna was pissed, that was for sure. Her usually precise speech always lapsed into the Deep South gumbo whenever she was angered, and I had always calculated my limits with her based on her diction.

"You best get outta that bed right now fo' I pulls you out. Hear me? Now get goin'."

I got going, her muttered invective following me down the hallway toward the bathroom. She was still mumbling to herself in a tone and attitude straight out of *Gone with the Wind* as I came out, went back to my room, and shut the door with as close to a bang as I dared. As I dressed I could hear her bustling about upstairs, still muttering but with her voice at times louder and at times softer. I could make out only a few words. All morning she was like that. A thirty-minute chat on the phone with one of her friends did little to alter her state of mind.

When the doorbell rang, she was standing at the sink, washing the same spoon over and over. The bell rang again. As I passed the open kitchen door on the way to answer the front door, she shot me a mean look.

I thought I understood her to say, "…ain't gonna tolerate it… not so long as there's breath left in this black body…"

Lunch was slammed on the table, and if looks could kill, Mark was being drawn and quartered and readied for burning at the stake.

"Aren't you going to join us?" I asked.

"Nossir, I ain't. I got other things to do."

But instead of going off to do those other things, she stood glowering in the doorway. Finally, she snatched the dirty dishes from the table and stalked into the kitchen and, we thought, out of earshot.

"What's her problem?" Mark asked. "She's mad as a hornet. You been giving her trouble?"

"She's been this way all morning ever since I told her you were coming for lunch."

"I thought she said it was all right."

"She did. Until I told her it was you coming."

"Why?"

"She thinks it 'don't look right.'"

"What doesn't look right?"

Miz Edna answered loudly from the kitchen.

"A grown man yo' age runnin 'round with a fifteen-year-old boy while his folks is gone."

Mark's face reddened.

"What business is that of yours?"

Miz Edna returned in fine fury.

"I'm responsible for a whole lot mo' 'roun here than washin' dirty dishes an' mor'n that I'm responsible to the Lord. An' this ain't right and you know what I'm talkin' about. An' me? I'm stayin' right here 'til this boy's folks comes to get him."

Mark rose.

"Excuse me, Allen. I'm leaving. Thank you for lunch, Miz Wilson. It was delicious. And informative. But I think you have overstepped your bounds."

Miz Edna fairly screeched.

"Don't you try an' be no white boy on me, Mr. Levy, Suh. You wanna call it 'white' you go ahead, and I know a plenty of Black folks that'd be glad to agree. Fact is, though, I've seen yo' kine in ever class of folk. Now, get thee behind me, Satan!"

I was shocked. I wasn't exactly sure I was following all of what she was saying, but I had only seen Miz Edna this mad once before. I never knew what had happened that time, but I knew not to ever make mention of it from my parents' dictum when they talked to me and Linda about it afterwards. And I was always frightened when Black folks took to testifying.

Mark quietly replied, "I meant no such thing, Miz Wilson. I am sorry you suspect my intentions. Good day."

Without checking to see what her reaction was, I followed Mark outside.

"Wait! Just wait! I'll talk to her."

"No. I've caused enough trouble already. Just let me go on. I've got things to do now, and quickly."

He jerked his arm from my grasp.

"Mark, will you just listen to me a second?"

"What? While she calls out the Lord's lynch mob?"

"Look. Just trust me. I think I can handle this. Give me half a chance, anyway. Please?"

He was crying. He nodded, and sat down on the steps, his head resting on his arms crossed across his knees.

Miz Edna was standing in the door.

"Get yo' lil butt in here!"

She grabbed me by the back of my neck in that authoritative manner as effective now on the cusp of manhood as it had ever been. She slammed the door closed.

"Miz Edna," I said from the couch where she had all but thrown me. "I know what you think and it's not true."

She towered above me, her hand making involuntary jerks.

"If it's not true then how come you know what I'm thinkin'?"

"Linda told me."

As hoped for, Linda's name worked its magic on Miz Edna. Her furor subsided rapidly and appreciably, though her words and voice remained condemnatory.

"Told you what?"

"That Mark's a queer."

"Don't you ever use words like that around me!"

She was steeling for another foray into righteousness. I knew I had better say what I had to say and say it fast.

"She's already told me about Mark and told me to stay away from him."

"Then what you doin' draggin' him in this house the first minute yo' mama's gone out of here? Thank the Lord Jesus Christ she ain't here to see it."

"I like him."

"What?"

"I like him. He hasn't touched me, made a move that direction, or anything of the sort. But I do like him. I didn't like him at first either, but give him a chance, Miz Edna. I swear I'll do nothing under this roof to cause you any problem with my folks. You have my word. Now, let me go out and take care of the rest of my problems. Please?"

I rose, hugged her, and kissed her on the cheek.

"Thank you Miz Edna. I won't let you down. I promise."

"I'm sorry, Baby." She patted my hand in hers. "I know you won't. I just forgot how much my little boy has grown up. I just got scared."

"Give me a couple of hours. And, look," I laughed, "go hit the liquor cabinet and tell Daddy I did it!"

She smiled.

"I know that's right!"

As I opened the door, Mark looked up with the eyes of a hunted beast.

"Move it, Jocko. You've got two hours."

He jumped up.

"What?"

"You've got two hours. Let's go."

"*Let's* go?"

"Yep. You got two hours."

"Before what?"

"Before I lose my chance and my nerve to convince you to lay me. There's just one condition."

He was staring with a mixture of confusion, amazement, and something resembling relief.

"What?"

"We can't do it here. I promised Miz Edna."

"You *what?*"

"Let's just get cracking. I'll explain on the way. Where are we going?"

CHAPTER 6

Mark called a friend. On the way to the friend's place, I explained the conversation with Linda and repeated what I had told Miz Edna. He just kept shaking his head, saying the same thing in any number of tonal and emotional variations.

"I don't believe this is happening. I just don't believe it!"

I laughed.

"You sound like you're trying to go your dad one better."

"Hunh?"

"You said the same thing a lot more times than twice. Don't you have anything else to say?"

"I don't believe this. I don't. I'm not putting my life on the line like this. This is a bad dream."

I fake huffed.

"Well, you can just let me out, if that's what you think."

"I don't believe this. I could wind up in jail the rest of my life if they don't hang me first. I must be crazy! I'm not going to do this. Let me just take you back home."

He turned onto a side street in preparation for retracing the journey.

"Hey! Quit wasting time. We've only got an hour and forty-five minutes left."

I reached to touch his leg.

"Don't do that here!"

"Then get me to some place private. You can waste time psychoanalyzing the situation if you want, but I'm ready *now*."

I laughed, but began unbuckling his belt to show my resolve.

"Christ! Cut it out!"

"Then let's go."

At the apartment door Mark removed an envelope from the mailbox. As he shook it to remove the key, something else fell out. I picked it up. It was a foil packaged condom.

Mark reddened.

"My friend thinks you're a woman."

"Oh."

We laughed and went in.

It is true that there are two things that can't be described, the sunset being one. But the earth moved!

I lay propped up on Mark's friend's pillow, watching as Mark was catching his breath. He had one hand cradling my head. I was tracing the outline of his nipple with my index finger,

"What time is it?" I asked.

"Oh, my God!" He jumped up. "I've got to get you home."

"No, you don't. Hold on."

I picked up the phone and dialed. A moment's wait.

"Hello. Miz Edna? I'm running a little behind. I'll be home in a little while."

A pause.

"No, no ma'am. Everything's fine. Okay. I'll tell him. I promise."

I hung up.

"She says she's sorry and asks you to forgive her."

"You're amazing."

"And you are, too!"

I leaned over to kiss him, moving my hand up his leg.

"God! You're gorgeous."

He pulled away.

"Look, we need to talk."

"Bullshit. We can talk later. Right now, I've got other things in mind."

I took the condom from the package and began to massage Mark.

The earth moved again, and this time, no doubt, registered somewhere near Golden, Colorado, where I envisioned some puzzled egg head in a white lab coat trying to decipher the meaning of these Richter registers from the Deep South. Was this another New Madrid quake? I laughed.

Mark, still laying atop me, asked, "What's so funny?"

I told him.

"You know something, Allen? You're weird. Always coming up with shit like that."

He started making moves to get up. I clamped my legs around him.

"Unh-unh. Stay here. You feel good."

He rolled off, tensed, and somewhat harshly spoke.

"Look, I'm sorry."

"Would you stop with all that guilt trip bullshit? Hey, Red Emma said it's okay, even with a rubber!"

I pulled his head upward by the hair at the back of his neck to where his face was now over mine. I kissed him again.

"Herr Doktor Freud, your little gris-gris worked. Now relax."

"What gris-gris?"

"Red Emma's sexual liberation gris-gris."

"You mean *that's* what brought this about? Lord, God! You *are* too taken by leftist politics, though I must admit, it's certainly a novel approach."

"No, that's not why I wanted to fuck you."

"It's not?"

"No. As you would say, it's much less 'prosaic.'"

"Do tell."

"You remember that day at the beach? Sunday, when we were getting ready to leave?"

"Yeah."

"And I was getting out of the water?"

"Yeah."

"You were staring at me. You stopped drying your hair, and just stared."

"You saw me?"

"Mmm-hmmm."

Mark was so serious when he spoke.

"I was scared shitless of you then."

"Yeah? Why?"

I tickled him, playing at the hair around his navel.

"I think I knew that sooner or later if I wasn't real careful, I was going to make a move."

"And that I would turn you down?"

"Or cause a scene."

"Why would I have done that?"

"Well, you don't seem to have a very high opinion of me."

"Okay, let me put it this way. I still think the Levys are bourgeois capitalist pigs, but Mark? Well, Mark's something else again."

I reached to grope him. He was still serious.

"Would you have turned me down?"

"Right then?"

"Yeah. If I had made a move right then."

"Nope. I wouldn't have."

"When did you change your mind?"

"Right then. When I got a good look at you."

"That's when I quit being a bourgeois pig?"

"Yep."

"And what am I now?"

"The most gorgeous thing I ever laid eyes on!"

"Thing?"

"Well, I don't know what men are supposed to say to other men."

"The same things they say to women."

"That seems, well, you know..."

"Queer?"

"Yeah. I guess." I laughed, paused, then added, "But I still more than likely wouldn't have. I don't know, on second thought, I probably would have turned you down."

"Why?"

I smiled.

"I hadn't talked to Linda yet."

"*What?*"

"I didn't know you were queer. I wouldn't have even known you were making a pass."

"Gay."

"What?"

"I'm gay,"

"Oh, yeah. I forgot."

"We'll talk about that later."

He rolled over.

"We better get cleaned up and dressed. We need to be gone before my friend gets back."

"And I'm not a woman."

"No. But you're one hell of a man."

I blushed. Mark noticed and laughed.

"You've got all the right equipment. You *sure* you've never done this before?"

"Swear to God."

"You sure learn fast."

"Hey, what can I say? I've got a good tutor."

As we were getting out of the shower, there came the unmistakable sound of the front door being unlocked.

"Oh, shit!" Mark muttered. "She's back already. I forgot I told her just a couple of hours. Oh, fuck!"

I joined him in the rush of buckles, buttons, and laces.

"What should I do?" I whispered.

"Just pray for the best."

Mark called to his friend.

"Sorry. We'll be out in a sec."

A cheerful, light voice called back.

"Take your time. I'll just put on some music. Y'all want some Chinese?"

We grimaced.

"No," Mark called though the door. "Thanks."

He took a deep breath.

"Let's get it over with. Shall we?"

I shrugged and followed him out the door.

"Christina," Mark called to a thirtyish, good-looking woman.

She turned, her face suddenly going from chipper to shocked.

"Christina Vickers, Allen Kramer. Allen, Christina."

I had to stifle a chuckle at the ever-so-proper etiquette given the situation. She looked quizzically from one of us to the other as I lamely made the social grace.

"Pleased to meet you."

She recovered.

"*Surprised* to meet *you*! Mark?"

"Well, uh, I've been meaning to talk to you."

"I wish you had've. It would've saved me a shock."

She flattened her palm over her breast in an exaggerated manner.

"I'm not sure my heart can take it."

"Let's sit down," he said, motioning me to sit next to him, putting his arm around me.

The situation was resolved quite smoothly amid jests and jibes. I quickly found myself warming to Christina. Her air, happy-go-lucky and matched to the sweetly timbered voice, put me completely at ease.

"I guess you didn't need my little present."

Mark coughed, somewhat embarrassed. I smiled broadly.

"Oh," she finished gamely. "Maybe you did. I won't ask."

I spent the next weeks finding ways to be alone with Mark. Anything was a possible excuse. We even went to Friday night services together as a prelude to, as the old folks used to say, making whoopee. True to my promise to Miz Edna, I "kept it out of the house." Miz Edna stayed silent on the matter, but erratically changed her hours about until I told her to quit trying to catch me doing something I had already promised her I wouldn't do. Mark kept his distance from the house.

My parents returned home, cheerful and souvenir-laden. Linda's postcards arrived periodically bearing exotic postmarks and stamps and full of wish-you-were-here. In occasional letters to me, she detailed her experiences with a not-so-holy yogi, a Soviet technician, and a Malaysian politician. The porch gatherings resumed and, aside from the time I was able to spend with Mark, life proceeded much the same as before.

I felt changed, and knew that it must show. It did. But the obvious change in my attitude set well with my parents. Much to Miz Edna's consternation they could not sing Mark's praises highly enough, something they apparently did all over the place. Even the rabbi was crediting Mark with a miracle.

Then, in late August, Mark dropped his bombshell. We were at Christina's place in the bed.

"It's time we talked, Allen."

"Okay. Talk."

"I'm not going to see you for a while."

"Why not?" I was stunned. "This is not some more of your guilt tripping, is it?"

"I'm going back Up North. To New York. I'm going to grad school."

"Oh," I said staring at the ceiling. "You picked a hell of a time and place to tell me, didn't you?"

"I started not to tell you at all."

"But your better nature got to you, right?"

"Look, I didn't promise you…"

"Fuck off."

"Hey, I thought at lest you would be glad I'm going to grad school."

"Glad? Is that what you said? 'Glad?' Oh, yeah. I'm just overjoyed. Motherfucker, do you think you can stroll in here, jump into bed with me, and then waltz out after rearranging my whole life?"

I began to cry. Mark put his arm around me, but I angrily shook him off.

"Die! Damn you! Christ! I hate you, you fucking asshole."

"Ssshh! Christina's got neighbors!"

"Fuck Christina and her neighbors, too! Hey, neighbors!" I screamed pounding the wall behind the bed, "Mark Levy is a fucking queer asshole!"

Mark's hand slammed into my mouth, splitting my lip. Enraged, I lunged at him. After a short struggle, he had my arm pinned behind my back, applying painful pressure. His other hand was clamped over my mouth. I was biting his flesh.

"Shut up, dammit! You're acting like a fool."

I struggled, but couldn't dislodge his grip. Finally I went limp. He turned my arm loose and after extracting a prodded promise from me to not yell, he removed his hand from my bleeding mouth. He looked at his bloodied, bleeding fingers.

"I didn't mean to hurt you, Allen."

"Well, I meant to hurt you, you motherfucking sonofabitch," I said in a quiet but venomous voice. "And I really thought…"

"Thought what? That I'd take you off on a white horse to a magic fairy castle somewhere and we'd live happily ever after?"

"Something like that, yeah!"

"Well, I won't. It doesn't exist. At least for people like us. Look, you've gotten it out of your system. I should never have let this happen, much less let it go this far. I'm leaving before…"

"Before what? Before you have to face reality, Baron von Levy? Run away to some ivory tower and write about adolescent development? What am I, some sort of class project? Or was I good enough to be a field experiment? You seemed to have no complaints long enough and often enough! Run out. Leave me. Just a summer fling. Christ! I sound like a bubble gum record!"

I began to dress. Mark made no move to try to stop me. He just watched. I reached for his pants, pulled his wallet out and, opening it, removed some bills. He still said nothing.

"Aren't you going to ask me what I'm doing, Mr. Klinkscales?"

"No."

"I'll tell you all the same. If I'm going to whore, then dammit, I'll get paid."

I opened the door, and Mark, still unmoving, followed me with his eyes as I closed the door behind me. The walk took most of two hours, and it was dark when I got home. A note asked me to call Christina.

I dialed the number from my room. She answered.

"This is Allen. You wanted me to call?"

"Yes. I wanted you to know if you need to let off steam, I'm here. That was a pretty shitty thing Mark did to you. He's a dickhead, and I told him so."

"Thank you, Christina. I appreciate it. Right now all I want is to crawl off in a hole somewhere, curl up, and die."

"Don't be…"

"Christina," I laughed, "not to worry. Suicide isn't Jewish! And besides if I ever do decide to do myself in, it'll be over something better than a shallow, self-serving fuck machine."

"That's a relief. But, I think you may be being a little hard on Mark."

"Look, just do me favor. You don't fall for some guy and him not have some redeeming qualities, but I don't want to hear it right now. He's dead for me, and I don't mourn his passing. I'll get over it. I've loved and lost before."

"Whatever you say, Sweet, but if you do want to talk, just call. That's what I'm here for. You're a sweet kid, and I don't want to see you get hurt."

"Honestly, I'm not hurt."

"Well, Mark is, and I think you might want to consider what this is doing to him."

"To *him?*"

"Yes, selfish child, to *him*. Have you given any thought to his position? Hell, think, dammit! He's twenty-one, and you're, what? Fifteen? And barely that! You may not want to believe it, but Mark doesn't go for boys. He's not a pederast."

"I suppose he told you that, and I suppose you believe him."

"Yes, he did. And I do."

"And this from somebody who didn't even know he was queer?"

"Gay."

"Oh, excuse me. Gay."

"Yes, I believe him. We talked a lot."

"You did? About me?"

"About you. And Mark. And me."

"You?"

"Yes, me."

"What's your interest in mine and Mark's bedroom?"

"I sleep in it more than you, for one thing."

I swallowed. In all of this I had not considered that Christina had been going way out on a limb out of friendship for Mark. I was willing to consider her, but not Mark's, feelings. In the mind's file labeled "Mark" there was only a void. A painful, aching void.

CHAPTER 7

My "mourning" was short lived. School was starting. Vietnam was becoming a cause even in our backwater, and I had found the protest movement. I was aware of the civil rights movement, but was not overly "taken with it." My parents were liberal on the issue which, in our town, meant not saying in public anything pro or con, yea or nay. I would come to learn that that, in and of itself, took a certain amount of courage. They were more outspoken on Vietnam and the subject was often the topic of dinner conversation at home. I slowly was beginning to realize that they were at last encouraging me in rebellion, and I, as they say, went "whole hog." I sewed the flag upside down on the seat of my pants. I wore black armbands. I read Ho Chi Minh and answered my teachers with quotes from Chairman Mao's *Little Red Book*. At school, there was a like-minded clique and we quickly fell to running together. There were protest rallies, marches, and underground papers to attend to. There was The Cellophane Sky where one could hang out, sometimes score the omnipresent mind-altering substances, and could discuss the novels of Hermann Hesse.

Mark Levy faded into the background.

Shortly after the start of classes, I got into trouble at school. With the help of the journalism teacher, our clique had taken over the school newspaper. The administration was proceeding with an expulsion edict from our defiance of an order to censor an article on venereal disease telling how to circumvent the state's parental consent law concerning treatment of minors. We had done an informational flyer and had distributed it to our classmates.

Strangely enough, my parents were backing me and with a few others we constituted a large enough group to keep pressure on the "pigs." But, the situation was threatening to get out of hand. The parents had gotten together and pulled in their clout with both respectable and radical lawyers alike studying the matter.

Then, in the middle of all this, the bastard showed up again.

As we were leaving services, Mark, home for the holidays, walked over to greet my parents and Linda.

Turning to me, he said, "You're getting to be quite the *cause célèbre*, you know that? They even know who you are in New York."

"I'm sure that no doubt they do. Liberals have a way of doing that."

"Still down on anything to the right of the Spartacists, are you?"

"You might say that."

He flashed that smile. I wanted to hit him in the mouth. Instead I bit into my lip.

"I'll call you," he said. "We'll talk about it."

I said nothing and walked, I hoped, nonchalantly to my parents' car.

Mark came over.

"Let me drive you home."

"Fuck off, pig!"

"Are we back to square one already?"

"No, we're not. This time I'm a little wiser."

He fumbled for a cigarette.

"Okay, I was a shit. I admit it. You scared the hell out of me, and I ran off. I made a mistake, and I know that now. I'd like to make it up to you…if I can…if you'll let me try."

"Why did you run off?"

"I told you. I was scared."

"Of what?"

He looked me square in the eye, his own eyes glistening.

"Of falling in love with you."

"Would that have been so terrible?"

"Yes, it would've. It was…it is…"

"What? What do you mean? What are you trying to say?"

"Running away didn't work. I did anyway, Allen. I do love you."

I hardened.

"You're a day late and a few shekels short. Sorry. But you missed your chance. But I have had time to think, and I don't…I can't…I won't hate you. Hate's too negative an emotion, and I really don't feel it."

"What do you feel?"

"Nothing. Just nothing."

"Come on, and let's go somewhere else," he said, nodding to my approaching parents.

"I've got to go now."

"No. Even if I have to drag you with me, Allen, I will. I'm not going to accept just that and nothing more."

I jerked away from him.

"Hold it, Buster. Can the shit. You've fucked me over one time too many already. Just leave me alone. I really don't need any more of this crap. And I really don't think a scene right here and now would do the Levy brand a lot of good."

"Fuck the Levy brand."

"I would've been a lot better off if I had done that instead of fucking Mark."

"Touché."

I turned once more to go, and Mark again caught my arm. He hissed in my ear.

"You can feel nothing if you want to, you little asshole, but I *do* feel something. And you're going to hear it. One way or the other."

"Sure. Whatever you say," I said, glancing over to check my parents' progress. "Just turn me loose."

"Will you go with me, then?"

"Okay. Whatever. Talk 'til you're blue in the face for all I care."

"Mr. Kramer," Mark addressed Daddy. "Do you mind if I bring Allen home later? I'd like to talk to him about some things if you'll let him go."

"Sure. Just be home early, Allen. You've got chores to do in the morning."

He turned to Mama, with that ever-so-deferential air.

"Miz Kramer, I know it's Friday, but this is something I really do need to talk to Allen about."

Mama, of course, was taken in.

"Oh, please don't worry about it."

Mark drove toward the freeway, only occasionally glancing to where I sat absently viewing the passing buildings. Outside the city he took an exit, and soon we were parked on a country road somewhere unrecognizable.

"All right," I said as he cut off the engine. "You win. I have no choice but to listen to you. I have no idea where I am."

"Fine! Just shut up and listen to me."

"Sure. Whatever."

I stared into the moonlit distance.

"Okay. I don't expect you to listen, but you will *hear* it. I don't go around molesting children, you know."

60

"Yeah. That's what Christina said."

"Well, I don't. I've never in my life done anything like that. My mistake was in forgetting that you are still a child. I..."

"Save the speech on my maturity, all right? I know what you're getting at."

"No, you don't. You just think you do."

"Oh? Then please 'educate' me, Mr. Levy. Just what do I not know?"

"That I love you."

"Oh, please! Am I supposed to melt now or later?"

"Neither one. I realize that now. I don't know what I was expecting. You...you..."

"I...I...what?"

"You've gotten next to me."

"Oh, so that's why you ran off? If that's your idea of what love is, I want no part of it."

"Okay. If that's the way you want to play, Mr. Perfect, then you tell me. What would you have done in my position?"

"I'd've never gotten in your position. I'd never have put up with me long enough."

"What?"

He seemed honestly puzzled.

"Mark," I said turning to face him, "I did think about this. It's really my fault, you know. I made the first move. It was my idea. I'm the one who held *your* hand. I'm the one who convinced you to...well...you know."

He was silent a minute.

"I know. I thought you were sure of it. I thought I was dealing with an equal. I lied to myself. I convinced myself that you were old enough to handle it because you were old enough to start it. You're right. I was the one who wasn't ready. But...I had to get away. I had to think, Allen."

He paused. I knew he was searching for the words to say what it was he had to think about. I certainly didn't expect what came next.

"I want you to come to New York."

I laughed with exaggerated sarcasm.

"Oh, sure. I'll go home and pack right now. I'll tell my folks I'm running off with my boyfriend to the big city. And they'll say, 'sure. When do we get to meet the young man?' Boy, you're a piece of work if ever there were. You're plumb insane!"

"I think I can convince your folks."

"Sure. I'm sure you could. That'd be really easy for you, wouldn't it? Flash that Levy charm. Lay on a heavy dose of 'he needs a guiding hand' big brother shit. Then bamboozle them with some psychological voo-doo. They'll fall for it. They already think you walk on water. They'd be more than happy to give you their little male child, too. And why not? They were ready to give you their girl child. Sure. Why not? Let's go."

"I'm serious."

"Oh, I know. That's what scares me. You're so fucking serious you probably could pull this off. I ought to say 'yes' just to watch your moves. You know something? You're a real sicko."

"No, I'm not."

"Oh, but you are."

"Did you think those days at Christina's were sick?"

"Not then."

"But you do now?"

"Yes. Yes, I do."

"Why?"

"Mark, you're 21-fucking-years-old. I'm still a kid. Okay? I was intrigued enough by the idea to consider it. I did it. I'm not sorry. But I'm not queer. I like girls. Got that? I know that now. I'm normal."

"And I'm not?"

"No. You're not. You're a pederast."

"And that makes you a victim, right?"

"Right."

"And you believe that?"

"I said it."

"But do you really believe it?"

"Yes. Yes, I do. You took advantage of me. Of my inexperience."

"I did? I asked you to go running off and find us a place to…?"

"Stop it. You know what I mean. You're the shrink."

"I know what you're trying to do, and it won't work."

"Oh? What *am* I trying to do?"

"You're trying to lay all the guilt on me. Remember who harped on and on about 'fucking guilt trips?' No, Allen, you're too smart for that. You're trying to exculpate…"

"Ex what?"

"Exculpate."

"What the hell does that mean?"

He smiled.

"Get rid of the blame."

"So, that's what you think I'm doing?"

"Trying to. Among other things."

"Such as?"

"Such as make me suffer. Hurt me. Make me feel dirty."

"I'll buy that."

"Well, I won't let you."

"Try and stop me."

"No. No, I won't. Do whatever you feel like. I just wanted to say…"

He started the engine.

"You wanted to say what?"

"That I really do care about you. That, as 'sick,' as you put it, as it may look, I really, honestly, care about you. And that's why I left. So I could work that out. To get away from it for a while. To see how I really felt. To get help if need be. And…"

"And what?"

"And to see if maybe you felt there was a chance…"

"For what?"

"To try to make some sense of this mess. If maybe, just maybe, you cared about me. But now I can see you don't." He jerked the car into gear. "I can see it's been a waste of time."

"Yes, it has been."

Mark drove back in silence.

At the house, Mama asked me, "Why didn't you invite Mark to come in?"

"I did, but he had to get home. He told me to ask y'all to excuse him."

"Come on down to the den. Your father and I want to talk to you."

My father switched off the television, nervously fiddling with the cigarette lighter he held in his hand.

"Sit down, Son."

The tone was that unmistakable "this is serious."

Nothing could have prepared me for what came next, considering what I had just left.

I followed his order. The opening seemed, well, 'normal' enough.

"You're staying in trouble. Your grades have been falling."

"But, Daddy, you know that…I thought you and Mama were behind me!"

Then he dropped the bombshell.

"We are, Son, but we think it may be good for you to get away for a while. This is not the place…you…we…this is a very conservative town and…well, we stand out…we're not like the others…"

"You're saying if we weren't Jewish?"

"No. Well, yes. But it's more than that. All this stuff you're getting into. We've got to think of your future. There'll come a time when you'll understand better."

"Daddy, what are you trying to say?"

"Your mother," he said looking over to where she sat silently, her eyes downcast, "your mother and I think it might be best were you sent to a boarding school away from here, and…"

"Military school? No! I won't!"

"Hon," Mama spoke at last. "No, not a military school. Your father and I think…"

Dad pulled himself up, his voice more resolute.

"We think you'd be better off Up North in a better school and among people with less conservative views. We want you to think about it. We're not trying to push anything on you, you understand. But maybe if you were to spend some time with Jake and Bess. They…they agreed for you to come up there."

"So, y'all've already decided."

"No, Son. We've not made any decisions of any kind. It's just a possibility."

"I don't want to. I like Uncle Jake and Aunt Bess, but I don't want to go there. I do understand what you're saying, though. Let me think about it for a while. Just not Uncle Jake and Aunt Bess. Okay?"

I didn't think about it for long. Uncle Jake and Aunt Bess lived in New York. The hand of Machiavelli Levy was evident.

CHAPTER 8

I looked out the window at the fresh and as yet untrodden snowfall. I had been here for only a couple of months, but was already writing home to my parents thanking them for the change, not just of scenery, but of attitude and with it a certain peace of mind. The boarding school was far from military. And despite the regimentation, I began to accept the idea of being alone in my room with my books. I held myself aloof from the other students, somewhat angered and somewhat amused by their fascination with my Deep South accent and by their bewilderment that I didn't fit their stereotypes.

Mark had written several long letters full of offers for me to come down from Vermont or for him to come up. I kept them, but didn't answer them. He was from that other life as far as I was concerned, as distant as Miz Edna's pralines and the azaleas Mama said were starting to bloom. Secretly now, though, I was beginning to long for those things of home, and more often lately the memories of those days with Mark came to my conscious thoughts, mixed in with thoughts of jambalaya and the giant oaks along the river bluffs. Homesickness. I'd be going home soon for spring break and Passover. I would be able to walk along the river in the warm sun. Miz Edna would fix me a pot of jambalaya. I smiled at the thought of her making sure it was kosher for Passover and how she, if not the rest of us, made sure the rules were obeyed and was grateful for the Sephardic laxity in matters of beans and rice. Mark would then vanish from my memories.

A knock at the door interrupted my reveries. The housemother handed me a note. I thanked her and closed the door, lying on the bed, and opened the envelope. I recognized Mark's handwriting.

"I'm in town. I want to talk to you about something important that I think you should know. Please call me."

There was a phone number. Instinctively, I threw the note aside, cursing the man under my breath. I tried to read, but couldn't. I turned on the stereo and put the earphones on. I smoked part of a joint. Still I was bothered. The images came and went. Mark at the beach. Mark lying in Christina's bed. Mark flashing his smile at me over cups of coffee. Mark slamming tennis balls my way.

I retrieved the note from where it landed when I had thrown it. I picked up the phone and dialed. I hung up. I dialed again.

Mark answered.

"Allen?"

"What do you want?"

"I want to talk to you."

"Fine. Talk."

"I want to see you."

"I don't want to see you. Say what you have to say, be done with it, and leave me alone."

"I want to tell you face-to-face."

"I don't want to see you."

"Look, asshole, I drove all the way up here in a blizzard to talk to you, and I'm not leaving until I do. I'm coming to get you. Be ready. I'll be there in about ten minutes."

He hung up before I could answer back.

Ten minutes later, the housemother was calling me to the common room.

Whatever resolve I may have had earlier was challenged at the first sight of him. He was more beautiful than I remembered. The northern winter clothes, rather than hide his beauty, only accentuated it. He stood nervously pulling his gloves from hand to hand, his head slightly bowed. When he looked up I saw in his eyes the same look he had that day last summer on the porch. He made to take a step forward, then faltering, stepped back. The housemother left us alone.

"Can we go somewhere to talk?" He asked

"Here's fine. Say what you have to say."

"All right then. I'm getting married."

I laughed at him.

"Married? To what?"

"A very nice girl."

"No doubt. And does this very nice girl have a name?"

"Sarah. Sarah Jean Hershkowitz."

"Oy! Sarah Jean *Whats*kowitz?"

"Hershkowitz. Be nice. You might try 'congratulations.'"

"Mazel tov, Old Man! Your life is now complete."

"I wanted you to know ...I want...I want you to be my best man."

"Whoo-ee! This is rich! Man, you have at long last completely lost all sense of rationality! What the hell..."

The housemother peeked around the corner.

Turning to her, I laughed.

"Excuse me, Mrs. Callahan. My confirmed bachelor friend here has just announced his defection to the ranks of the normal."

She smiled tautly.

"Congratulations, young man."

She returned to her business.

"Form above substance at all times, eh, Mark? How much did your old man promise you to marry her? Or was it her old man's dowry? I'm sure there's got to be some monetary reward of some kind in there somewhere."

"I like her. I may even love her, and you're right. It is for form's sake. I want children."

"I bet you do! Not having any luck with other people's and decided to have some of your own? I hope you have a son who looks just like you. Then you can really go fuck yourself, which is what you'd really like to do anyway."

He didn't respond to that, and what he did say caught me off guard.

"She knows about you."

I shook my head.

"You know something? You're nothing short of amazing. You know that? So, tell me, how did Princess Manischewitz take the news?"

"She wants to meet you."

"She what? Where did you find this gem? Bellevue?"

"Sort of."

"No doubt. Well, tell her I don't think that'll be possible. I'd certainly like to *see* her, though. I'll bet she's a pip."

"You might be surprised."

"No doubt."

"Would you like to meet her? Give her a chance?"

"It seems I've heard that line somewhere before. No, I don't think so if it's all the same. But I am interested in what's won your attention over me. Check out the competition, so to speak."

He pulled his wallet from his pocket and showed me a picture. She was beautiful, elegantly dark-haired with intelligent, far-away, green eyes.

"She looks like Scarlet O'Hara sans the fire. Y'all ought to look just perfect together. Tell me where she's registered and I'll send an ever-so-tasteful gift."

"Allen, please meet her. For me."

"For you?"

"For me. She wants to understand that part of me. To try and understand what it is between two men. To understand why I love you the way I do."

"Oh, I get it. Kink. Tell you what, I'll just pop on down to New York, and we can get it on for her, all right. Butt fuck. Suck cock. I mean, you know, do it all. Sure. Let's give the girl a real education."

"Shut up. I'm serious."

"So am I. Seems like I remember you telling me one time that two men are no different than a man and a woman. Run that up the pole and see if she salutes."

"I want her to *see* that."

"Just what did you tell her about me?"

"That you were sweet, smart, kind, beautiful, and the only man I have ever loved."

"And she bought that, did she?"

"Yes."

"Boy, she must be something!"

"She is. She's understanding."

I thought for a minute.

"You know something, Mark? This is so perverse, it's tempting. I'm tempted just to see what happens. Who knows? She might like it so much she'd kick you to the curb and try to knock off a piece of me. After all, keep it in the family."

He looked up.

"Are you serious?"

"Christ, no!"

"Think about it. Let's…will you go to dinner with me this evening?"

"Are you asking me for a date?"

"No. Just a favor."

"Why not? I don't know anybody here. I could use a free meal, and this could be material for a trashy novel someday. Yeah. Sure."

When he left I tried to think of what to say, how to approach the question. Did I want to do what he was asking? Why would I, I thought. This was just too out there. Best man? I laughed out loud at the idea. But still, I couldn't help thinking that there was in it some kind of compliment, however bizarre.

Dinner was uneventful. Pretty much two old chums from the same home town catching up on the banalities with idle chat. In the end, I made up my mind to meet Sarah Jean. When I got back to my room, I called my parents to tell them that I'd be coming home a few days later than planned. Mama answered. I was relieved. Best to get the hard part out of the way first.

"But, Honey, we've got everything ready."

"I'll be home for Passover. I just need to be in New York for a couple of days."

"Why can't it wait?"

My Dad broke in.

"Oh, don't be silly, woman. Who is she, Son?"

"Sarah Jean Hershkowitz. But she's not mine. She's Mark Levy's."

"Pardon?"

"Mark's getting married, and he's asked me to be his *shomer*. I'm going down to meet her, and then I'm riding down with them. She's coming to meet his folks."

Mama rattled off into a thousand questions, ending with "do his folks know?"

I laughed.

"I have no idea, but it's best not to say anything just in case. And Mama, for goodness sakes, please don't tell Miz Santo or Miz Feinstein!"

I caught the late bus into the city the Friday before break. Mark met me. His fiancée was absent.

Breaking the gentlemanly handshake, I asked, "Well, where is the new Mrs. Levy-to-Be?"

"You'll meet her tomorrow. She's not able to make it today. She sent this."

He handed me an envelope.

"Dearest Allen," I read aloud. "Please forgive me for not coming to meet you. I have to be at the hospital. Please accept my apologies, and I look forward to meeting you tomorrow. Yours, Sarah Jean."

I folded the note and put it back in its envelope.

"How very sweet, and so proper. Hospital?"

"She's a resident. At Bellevue."

"Oh. I see. A resident? Physician or inmate?"

"Last year physician. Actually, psychiatrist."

"A Yankee voo-doo doctor?"

"Her words exactly. She's from New Orleans."

"Okay. Looks like I've really fallen into a den. Last year of residency? She's a lot older than you."

"A few years. Not a *lot*."

"Younger man, older woman. Boy, you do have your ways. Well," I said picking up my bag, "let's get the show on the road."

Outside Mark hailed us a cab and gave the cabbie an address. We settled in for the ride.

"Where are we going?"

"To my place."

"I'm staying there with you? Alone?"

"Yes."

"Empty form at all costs. Separate beds?"

"Separate accommodations."

The cabbie looked around. Mark addressed him.

"Just drive."

"Hey, Mack, who am I to knock it? Just don't let the juvenile authorities get wind of it. They're rough on that kind of thing up here. This ain't Alabama."

"I know," Mark replied. "People in Alabama mind their own goddamn business."

"Hey," I said. "Cool out. Let's talk about something else."

"Okay. How's your party life?"

"I stay in my room."

"Not that kind. *The* party."

The cabbie looked back at us in the mirror. I laughed.

"I've quit the party. They can't dance."

From there the conversation flowed more smoothly into a pleasant interlude of back home, nostalgic camaraderie. Mark did his impression of Mrs. Feinstein hearing the news of his upcoming marriage. The conversation ended as Mark unlocked his apartment door.

This was the first time I had seen Mark in his own environment, his comfort zone. The two rooms were Spartan. The only signs of wealth and luxury were the stereo system, shelves and shelves of books, and two oil portraits which immediately caught my eye. They were of rabbis and beautifully executed in the style of the late 19th Century. I went over for a closer look.

"I got these from Sarah Jean. They're of a great-uncle of hers and her great-grandfather. She brought them back from Poland."

"What?"

73

"The Polish government tracked down the owners. They wrote the family and told them that unless they came to Poland to reclaim them that they would become property of the state. Sarah Jean went to get them. Nobody else in the family wanted them."

"They're wonderful. It's hard to believe…"

"What?"

"That that world is gone. Wiped out. It is no more."

He laughed.

"Almost. I'll take you to see the Hassidim. They look just like Bert and Ernie."

"Who?"

"Bert and Ernie. Our names for Izzie and Abie. Want to freshen up?"

"Yeah. And then to get some sleep. Where do I do both?"

He pointed to the bathroom, throwing me a towel.

"Couch or bed?"

"Whichever."

"I'll make the bed for you. It'll be more comfortable. Don't fret. I'll take the couch."

I showered and came back into the living room, a towel wrapped around my waist, running my hands through my hair. Mark looked up from the book he was reading.

"You're filling out. Lifting weights?"

"Nope. Swimming. I'm getting ready to challenge you again."

He sat staring as I pulled my pajamas from a bag.

"Excuse me," I said as I went back to the bathroom to put them on.

When I came back, Mark was stretched out on the couch.

"You didn't have to do that, you know," he said.

"Do what?"

"Go in there to change. I've seen you naked."

"Right. And we know what happened. No way. We'll just keep this nice and safe. You keep your distance, and I'll keep mine."

"If that's the way you want to do it."

"It's not a matter of whether or not I want to," I said, allowing myself to look at his naked torso above the blanket. "It's a matter of what I am going to do."

CHAPTER 9

I slept soundly with no dreams and no restlessness. I might as well have been in my own room instead of passing the night in my old boyfriend's bed, waiting to meet his fiancée. I woke to Mark's shaking me. Blinking my eyes against the bright sunlight from the window, I saw Mark dressed as always with every detail just perfect.

"You need to get up. It's past ten, and we're meeting Sarah Jean at noon for lunch."

He stroked my hair back from my forehead.

I pulled back.

"A quickie before meeting the wife for lunch? You've really got this all arranged, haven't you?"

He lit a cigarette, staring into the smoke as he exhaled watching the changing patterns in the light before he spoke.

"Yes. I have it all arranged. Right on schedule. Just perfect. No flaws. No fuck-ups. Everything just like it's supposed to be. Get dressed."

He turned and walked to the kitchen area, calling back to me too lightly to be real.

"Two creams, no sugar. Right?"

"You remembered. How sweet."

He returned with the coffee.

"I remember it all. Every moment of every day. Didn't you get the letters?"

"I got them."

"But you didn't read them?"

"I read them."

"Then why didn't you answer them?"

"I didn't have anything to say."

He sprawled into a chair, his legs stretched out before him, hands behind his head.

"And I'm supposed to be wounded by that?"

"If that's the way you want to take it."

"You fucking bastard," his voice hardened. "Do you know how hard it was to write those letters? To try to come to terms with..."

"Your 'feelings'?"

"Yes. My feelings."

"Well, why didn't you just run away again? It must be easy for a Levy."

"So. We're back to that again, are we?"

"Aren't we?"

I got up and began to rummage through my bags for my clothes.

"I mean, after all, we are off to meet the incubator for the continuation of the line, aren't we?"

We both looked at the portraits at the same time in that calm quiet which seems to last for a long time, but really lasts for only a few seconds.

Mark broke the silence.

"But it's more than just duty. You'll see when you meet Sarah Jean."

I believed him. I thought for a minute that I understood that damnable curse to procreate. I understood, I thought, the meaning of the exile from Eden.

I dressed. We went out. We met Sarah Jean at a place which was what I had expected. Not too formal, not too relaxed. Not too expensive, but not an embarrassment on the credit card statement.

Sarah Jean was pleasant. Too pleasant. Like Mark, she was a study in perfected moves. Her speech with that distinctive gentleness unique to New Orleans lulled me by its cadence into a security of comfort, the words and their meanings lost in the sensuality of their sounds. The arrival of the food jarred me back into reality.

"Mark says you read."

"I do know how to."

She laughed easily.

"He also says you're a wise ass."

"He knows the area well."

She looked down at the plate. Mark spoke, his voice angry.

"That's not necessary."

With more sincerity than I would have willed, I apologized.

"I'm sorry. Please forgive me. It's just...well, I'm..."

She smiled.

"Not sure how to act? Me either. I thought I was ready for this."

"But?" I asked.

"You're sitting there, and I'm sitting here. This is not what I thought it would be. Nothing I practiced saying will come out. You're so...so..."

"Young?"

"No. I expected that. How do I say it? I understand a little better after seeing you."

"What does that mean?"

"You're so beautiful. I know that's the word I want, but..."

"But what?"

I was thinking here comes the *ménage à trois*. She reddened, as if reading my thoughts.

"I don't mean that. I mean your eyes. Your hands…"

"I have two of both. Just like normal people."

It was Mark's turn to stiffen.

She continued.

"No. I was *expecting* normal. They're not normal. They're different. Mark didn't warn me."

"Warn you?"

"Yes, warn me."

She took one of my hands in hers.

"They're like a sculpture. But the eyes. What *do* you know that the rest of us don't?"

She paused, and smiled gently.

"I'm embarrassing you. I'm sorry."

We ate in silence for several minutes. The sounds of silverware against china, the tinkle of glass, the muted conversations of the people around us, all sounded, it seemed, as loud as a bottle rocket. Still, Mark and Sarah Jean kept their composure. I fidgeted. I dropped my napkin. Sarah Jean broke the silence.

"How are you liking your new school?"

"Fine."

We ate on. At length Sarah Jean spoke.

"This is uncomfortable for both of us."

She moved as if to leave. Mark reached his hand to touch her arm, holding her back. At the same time I heard myself speak.

"Don't go."

She looked quickly back and forth between Mark and me, her eyes questioning, with an almost helpless, hunted look.

"Sarah Jean," I said, "let's just go ahead and get this over with. Why are you marrying him?"

"We love each other."

I laughed.

"And it's okay with you that he's queer."

"Gay."

"Okay. Gay. Queer. Homo. Anyway, he likes boys, not girls."

"And you never 'liked' a girl?"

I hesitated, then said nearly spluttering.

"Yes. I like girls, not boys."

"But you slept with Mark?"

"Well, that's a different story. He..."

"*He*? I thought," she looked not at Mark, but directly into my eyes, "that you were the one who made the first move."

Mark was looking down at his plate, like some guilty child, playing with his peas. I felt the anger rise.

"That depends on what you mean by the first move," I fairly spat out. "That damn tennis match wasn't *my* move. Neither was going camping."

I paused, catching my breath before continuing.

"And I certainly didn't go talking to *his* parents about *his* problems."

"Did he do that to you?"

"Oh, he didn't tell you that, I'm sure. All that big brother happy horse shit. All that...that...I don't know what you'd call it. Mark? What *would* you call it? 'Counseling?' Or maybe 'seduction?' Or better yet, let's just call it what it was, 'pederasty.'"

Sarah Jean's laughter caught me by surprise.

"Pederasty?"

"Yes."

"Oh, my. Such a word coming from you. I expected something a bit more original and not so technical."

"What term would you use for him, then?"

"Smitten."

"What?"

"Smitten. With good cause. And what would you call yourself? A victim? Accomplice? Look at him."

I didn't move.

"Look at him, dammit!"

Without moving more than my eyes, I looked at him.

"Good. See him? What do you think you did to *him*? You mean to tell me he's nothing to you? Or did you just play him like a harp to find out about men? Why him? So he's nothing to you. You have no feelings toward him?"

"None whatsoever."

Mark spoke.

"I'm sorry for all this. I wanted you to stand there with me. My 'best' man. I wanted…but, who cares? It doesn't matter. If you won't do it…"

"Who said I won't do it? I wouldn't miss this freak show for the world."

"What? You will?"

Sarah Jean smiled.

"Thank you."

"Empty form above all, eh Mr. Levy?" I said raising my glass. "To you and the continuation of a fine line of court Jews."

I had decided not to ride down with Mark and Sarah Jean. The idea of being closed up in a car for 24 hours with them had no appeal and promised to be a social situation I simply was not ready for. Truth be told, they probably were relieved themselves.

Sarah Jean had "insisted" that I not change the plans.

"It would give me and Mark somebody to bore besides each other."

"I doubt you two are boring."

"More than you'd ever believe."

Mark made his own pro forma "it would be nice if you would."

And of course, I had to join them with my own "excuses."

"I really wish I could, but Mama was sort of let down that I wasn't coming down as planned. They already had my ticket."

"We understand," Sarah Jean said. "At least let us drive you to the airport. When is your flight?"

"Six."

"Tonight or in the morning?" Mark asked.

"Tonight. So don't worry. You can have your bed back and not have to sleep on the couch."

I noted Sarah Jean noted that and noted that Mark noted that she noted. My point. I'm sure they also noted me note them noting.

She accompanied us back to Mark's apartment to collect my things. As we were getting ready to leave, I went over, I guess you could say, to tell Bert and Ernie farewell. Sarah Jean joined me, looking at me look at them.

"The great-grandfather died before the war. The great-uncle," she nodded her head to the younger of the two, "we think was killed at either Belzec or Sobibor. We're not sure which."

She looked at me, at the portrait, then back at me.

"He has your eyes."

I was relieved on the flight down to find that my seatmate was returning from a business trip and, pleasantries exchanged, excused himself to "catch 40 winks before having to be at work in the morning." I read a few pages of the book I had brought along, picked at the airline food, and the tray collected, let my seat back, grateful that the seat behind me was unoccupied.

The portraits stayed with me, especially the one of the great-uncle. What was his experience? What did he go through? Did he have a wife and children, grandchildren, brothers and sisters, nieces and nephews, cousins, friends, neighbors whose portraits, photographs, letters, any record of their existence gone into the flame? What were his joys, his sorrows? How could this have happened to any people, but to *my* people?

My people? Were they really? For the first time, I really thought about that. About what it meant to be a Southern Jew, or was I a Jewish Southerner? My ancestors, like Mark's, had been in the South since the 1700s. They had been there for the American Revolution, the Civil War. The endless pogroms were something that for generations had been happening elsewhere to another people in another land.

But, yes, they were *mine*, too, and in a few days, I would be sitting not just with my own family but with my people around the world, performing the same rituals, asking the same questions, thinking of what it means to belong to something which was there long before you came and would be there long after you were gone. What, exactly, did this "chosen" thing mean? What was this "thing" that made us, *me*, different? That thing that only those "like" you could understand?

CHAPTER 10

The Levy wedding was the talk of the side porch. Every detail was rehashed and served for leftovers for weeks. The Hershkowitz Girl's family tree was analyzed to exhaustion. The gifts were evaluated for dollar value and taste. The "pieces" from the famous Levy collection were of special interest, Mrs. Levy's opinion of her new daughter-in-law being gauged by the choice of heirlooms.

"You know," Miz Santo said, helping herself to a third praline from the tray, "the Levys don't have any other children, and I've always wondered where those things would go. I was afraid that they'd be sold, and I always told Mr. Santo…"

And the conversation moved on into the matter of the election primaries and which candidate's wife was the best candidate for first lady of the state. I lay on the chaise lounge in the backyard, listening to the lulling drawls, my mind's eye recalling images from the "perfect" wedding.

The image which kept coming to mind was the toast from Mark to "two special friends who convinced us to get married, Bert and Ernie." A gale of laughter had followed, but Mark and Sarah Jean remained serious and looking at me.

That image persisted even when the other memories were dulled from the over recall in my own mind as well as the constant reminders from the side porch. I had tried to write to Mark and Sarah Jean, telling them that I thought I now understood their marriage, but each of the letters was in turn destroyed. Each time the words I wanted refused to come.

Summer day passed into summer day. I read. I took long walks. I got my driver's license and took long rides. The happy couple came home to visit before setting up housekeeping in New York. The yentas knew all of the details. Linda grimaced at their mentions of the "heirlooms" poor Sarah Jean would have to guard with her life until the day she could pass them on to the next generation. I managed to avoid "lunch."

I gave in and took Tuna Fish out. The yentas nodded their approval. Mr. and Mrs. Golden nodded their approval. The rabbi nodded his approval. Mama and Daddy smiled their pride at services. Miz Edna fixed us her best dishes. Great-Aunt Mildred increased her "gifts" for "you and your girlfriend to have a good time."

Rounds of gossip. Primary elections. Newlyweds doing well. The Levy Boy got a prestigious grant. The Levy Boy's wife is finishing up her residency. The Paris Peace Talks. Nixon. Watergate. The first semi-cool nights. Time to go back to school. Goodbye Tuna Fish.

I was packing my bags when Daddy came in.

"Son, I'm proud of you. You're turning out to be a fine young man. I want you to know that. We're proud. All of us. Me, your mama."

He paused.

"And Mark."

I looked up at him.

"Mark?"

"Especially Mark. He did a good job with you. I hope you appreciate it."

"Oh, I do. You'll never know just how much."

I slammed the lid shut on the suitcase.

"What's wrong, Son?"

"Nothing. It's just this thing is too full."

"You're upset, aren't you?"

"Nossir. Really. I just feel like…well, you know what it's like when you pack. You always forget something. Like you're leaving something important behind. That's all."

Daddy stood, hesitated, then hugged me.

"I'm going to miss you, Son. I wish you were here, but you…"

I smiled.

"Hey, don't worry about it. I understand. And believe you me, I *do* appreciate what you and Mama are doing for me. I know this is costing you money you could use elsewhere. I know you're doing what's best."

"Even if I am a capitalist pig?"

I laughed.

"Yessir, even if it is capitalist pig!"

He picked up the book by my bed.

"E. M. Forester, eh? I see your reading's changing. Have you read *A Passage to India*?"

I froze. I prayed silently that he wouldn't look too closely at the dust jacket. Why hadn't I removed it?

"He died not too long ago. I've never heard of this one. *Maurice*? I'll have to read it."

I breathed a sigh of relief as he put the book back on the nightstand.

"Get some sleep," he said. "I called Bess and Jake. They'll meet you at the airport. They're glad you decided to spend a few days with them."

"Well, I felt kind of guilty being up in Vermont and not getting down to see them. I hope they understand. It just took some getting used to."

"I know. Let me let you get to bed. Good night."

I left on Sunday. I called Mark on Monday. He sounded surprised.

"Can we get together?" I asked.

"When?"

"I'm here until Thursday."

"I'll pick you up tomorrow for dinner. Sarah Jean..."

"I don't want to see Sarah Jean."

"What?"

"Not *that*. I just have something I want to say to you. Something..."

"Personal?"

"Sort of."

"I'm out of class. How about let's play tourist tomorrow. We could..."

"No. I only need a few minutes."

"Oh. I see. Okay. Let's do lunch."

I laughed.

"Let's. Empty form above all, you know."

Another "nice" restaurant. Mark just perfect, unchanged, the same as always, though maybe only more distant.

"Well?"

"Well what?"

"Aren't you going to ask why I wanted to see you?"

"I figured you'd tell me when you were ready."

"I just wanted to let you know I think I understand why you got married. Bert and Ernie, right?"

"Right."

"I thought so."

"And?"

"And what?"

"That's all you wanted to say?"

"Yes. That's all. Except..."

I paused. He spoke.

"Except?"

"I'm glad you found someone who understands you. Who'll let you go your own way."

"Go my own way?"

"You know, have your night out with the boys, so to speak."

"There are no nights out with the boys."

"Oh, please."

"No, there aren't."

"So. You're reformed."

"No. I just don't want that. Not since you."

I laughed sarcastically.

"You expect me to believe that?"

"No."

He paused, and spoke quietly.

"No, I don't. I don't expect anyone to. But it's true."

"You're warped and twisted, Mark."

"Maybe. But I hope one day you'll understand."

"I doubt I ever will, my friend. But we'll see. You know, I have my whole life ahead of me and all that garbage. I've got to go."

I got up from my seat.

"Take care, Mark. I just wanted to let you know. Give my regards to your wife."

I walked out without looking back.

School began and with it the first cool days of fall. I took my placement exams. By doubling up, I would be able to graduate a year early, a fact I was sure would soon be the topic of conversation at the afternoon gatherings, the bridge table, and what-have-you. I watched the New England autumnal riot of color from my window over my desk.

Marx was replaced by calculus, Red Emma by physics, and Mark by long nights of symbolism in French literature. My grades were good. Life continued in its petty pace, and soon it was time for Thanksgiving break, a trip home, turkey and trimmings, back to school, mid-terms, and holidays again.

A few days before Christmas, I was at the mall catching up on the shopping I had put off. I was sitting in the food court, totally absorbed in the sensual pleasures of a hot sausage po' boy, relishing the spicy flavors so missed, when I was brought back to reality by the sound of someone calling my name. I looked up to see Sarah Jean.

As she approached, I stood, moving my packages for her to sit, kissing her proffered cheek.

"Home for break?"

"Yeah, getting some last-minute shopping done."

"Me, too. I've still got Mark's mother to buy for. I have no idea what to get her."

I smiled.

"How about a case of furniture polish?"

She laughed.

"I know that's right. The idea of another room full of that junk is terrorizing."

"Oh, so she's passing on by the room full now?"

"Well, I don't expect to get through this trip without it."

She mimicked Mrs. Levy's voice.

"Now, Darlin', you've got to take this crib. This'll be the fifth generation of Levys to sleep in it."

I was startled, and my surprise brought about a smile from her, a pat on the stomach, and the comment, "Three months."

"Congratulations. Y'all work fast, don't you?"

"Thank you. We decided to do this before I start my practice. Mark's excited. We're saving the announcement until New Year's. So don't let it out."

"Don't worry. I won't. I wouldn't have known if you hadn't told me. You can hardly tell."

"*I* can!"

We chatted a few minutes longer. Without Mark present, I realized that I probably would have liked Sarah Jean a lot.

I got through the holidays without seeing Mark. He called the house a couple of times, but I didn't return the calls.

CHAPTER 11

As I sat watching the snow swirl in the wind against the street lights, the phone rang. It was Daddy and, true to form, he got right to the point.

"Son, I've got a surprise for you. I know what winters up there can be like. Carnival is coming up and your Aunt Maude is refugeeing this year. She says that you kids can have dibs on her place. What do you say? Want to bring some of those poor, old, deprived Yankee boys down and show them how to have a good time? I promise you your mama and I'll stay away. Of course you and Linda know what's expected of you so far as respecting Aunt Maude and her house."

I laughed, visualizing the grin on my father's face.

"Don't we just!"

Aunt Maude was really my great-aunt on my mother's side. While her family was glad the old broad kept her distance, Daddy's family was proud to have her as extended and eccentric kin. Depending on how you looked at it, Aunt Maude was either Quarter trash or a Vieux Carré resident, not that she greatly cared. She counted among her eclectic set plenty of each. Aunt Maude was a grande dame of the old school who by her own admission had made a pleasure of business and vice-versa. She had been married five times, all of them rich, and all of them younger than her.

"I sucked them to the marrow and made gris-gris of the bones."

Her advice to Linda told a lot about her world view.

"Honey, as you know, love is like the dew. It is as likely to fall on a rose as a cow turd. It's been my experience that it is to your advantage to hang out in rose gardens and not cow pastures."

The residence being proffered she called la Maison du Turd de Vache and was left her by her first experience with the fall of dew in what she referred to as her "Mormon marriage." Most of us knew this gentleman only from legend, no small part of which was of Aunt Maude genesis. She had entered into the relationship young, innocent, and naïve.

"We could've waved the bloody sheet."

By that time, though, it was too late to go back, and there was nothing left to do but make the best of it.

Aunt Maude did just that, and she never spoke ill of his provender. She was of the opinion, and he agreed, that if the delicate flower of Southern maidenhood was to be a kept woman, then she would be kept in style. He bought her la Maison du Turd, and in it Aunt Maude lived the life of her dreams, figuring that if she was going to flout stuffy convention then she should look for role models. She found them among the Gallic salonistes, and New Orleans and the Vieux Carré gave her the stage on which to play her role and be respected.

Her business acumen and style combined to put her, as she said, "In the blessed position of being able to tell anybody, any time, any place to go to hell, and get by with it."

Daddy continued.

"So, Boy, what do I tell her? Will you come down and keep an eye on Maison du Turd?"

"Well, Pops, I'm short on cash."

"Oh, I forgot. She also says the trip's on her. Everything. Says she wants y'all to have a first-class blowout for her since she's too old to foxtrot anymore."

"How long has it been since she buried Uncle Hal?"

"I guess, what? About three years now? The longest time I've ever known her to be between men."

"Tell me something, Dad, what ever happened to Joseph Smith?"

"Son, that's for Aunt Maude to tell. Not me. And she'll tell you when she's good and ready."

"She better hurry. She's what? Eighty-three now?"

"Be 83 in May. Interested?"

I looked back out the window at the snow, and involuntarily shivered. A week away from that would be nice.

"Great. I'll see if I can find anybody who wants to come down."

"Find 'em? Boy, even a hermit monk like you shouldn't have any trouble finding a slew of folks ready to come to Carnival."

"You know, it's funny how when you grow up with something, it's hard to understand how other people see it. I remember when we were little and we were out on Aunt Maude's balcony. She said, 'Look at y'all. You don't even know you're privileged. Look at those folks down on the street, looking up at you like you're a prince and princess.' Then Linda said, 'yes ma'am. We know that. That's why we're throwing them beads.'"

Dad laughed.

"That balcony's still one of the best spots in the city for crowd-watching any time of the year. You get to see it all."

It was my turn to laugh.

"At Aunt Maude's you can do that without ever stepping out on the balcony!"

"Used to. Aunt Maude's almost closed up shop. Your mama says she's getting right with God, getting ready to die. But I think it's a little more earthly than that. The way I've got it figured is that she's found herself a 70 year-old lawyer or investment banker with a bad ticker and no heirs."

"We can hope! What does Mama have to say about this?"

"Oh, your mama of course doesn't like it. You know how her bunch is about Crazy Aunt Maude. But, I'd be a lot more worried if she *did* like it. Like Aunt Maude says, though, 'What the hell do I care about what she thinks? She's blood and there's nothing I can about that, but the only sign that chile ever showed that she was possessed of a glimmer of a light in her attic was when she married you. And it's probably a good thing she switched it off as soon as y'all were hitched.' You want to talk to your mama?"

He passed her the phone without waiting for an answer from me.

"Son? How are you?"

"Fine, Mama."

"How's school?"

"Fine."

"Your grades?"

"Fine, Mama. I'm eating properly, getting plenty of sleep, changing my underwear, take a bath like I'm supposed to, and there's no loose women in my life."

"But I worry about you, Hon."

"Mama, I'm glad you do, but really, my life is pretty boring. After all, there's not a whole lot of mischief you can get into in 20-foot snow drifts and -20 degree weather."

"You'd be surprised."

"I'd probably be shocked."

"So, Mardi Gras sounds like a good idea then. You're coming down?"

"Yes ma'am."

"Aunt Maude wants you to come straight down there and not stop by here for a few days. But I understand."

"Mama, aren't you and Daddy going?"

"Oh, we'll be in and out. Your Daddy finally won."

"You don't mean it!"

"He says with you kids gone now it's *our* time. So, if that's what he wants. But, a *houseboat*? I think his mama was scared by an alligator when she was carrying him."

"Where is it?"

"On some godforsaken bayou off Tabasco Road."

"You haven't seen it yet?"

"Oh, no, Dear Heart. This is late-breaking news around here. He came back from New Orleans the other day, papers in hand. Refused to let me see them or tell me where it was. He said he wanted me to be surprised. I'll bet."

I was laughing. Any time Daddy was stressed about something, he always claimed he was going to chuck it all and go live on a houseboat on the bayou.

"So, what else is news?"

"Nothing much. Ole Miz Weintraub passed. We sat shivah. Little Maggie Carlsson got married. Her husband's a good boy. He's a hard worker and will make something of himself."

My tone hid my smile.

"Not from a good family, eh?"

"You know I don't want to say something like that, but they are kind of new around here. They seem nice enough. They're from somewhere up in Ohio. They came in here to manage one of those new plants, and it's taken them a while to settle in. But, like I said, they seem nice enough."

"Yankees-but-not-goyim?"

"Now, I never said that either. But, well, yes. The mama stepped on some toes when they first got here, but that's to be expected. I speak to them at temple, and I've had her over for coffee a couple of times. Her husband works all the time, though."

"And life goes on."

"So it does. Let's see. That's deaths and marriages. That leaves births. No new ones. Your friends Mark and Sarah Jean are expecting, but I guess you knew that already."

I caught my breath.

"Genetically engineered with Mendel in mind."

"Now don't get started on all that. I can't for the life of me understand what it is you've got against the Levys. They're fine folks, and I don't see anything wrong with proper breeding. I certainly had that in mind when I chose your daddy."

"The sire, you mean?"

"If you want to put it that way, yes."

"So, I guess that makes you a brood mare, then."

"Well, do you have any complaints?"

I lightened up, envisioning just how serious Mama's face would look.

"Okay. Point made. If I were choosing egg and sperm, y'all ain't bad material! But, better be careful, it's Aunt Maude's blood, too. I may be a throwback on the genes."

"Well, if y'all are like her then it'd have to be the genes because you kids weren't *raised* to be like her."

"Mama, this is costing money, and I need to get back to the books. Yes ma'am, I'll be there, and no ma'am, I won't stop by y'all's place first. But I do want to see Dad's houseboat."

"Better bring your own pirogue. I love you, Son. Your daddy wants to say goodbye. Be good, and we'll see you come Carnival."

"Bye, Mama. I love you."

Dad came on.

"Okay, Boy, I'll tell Aunt Maude you want to come. Better, still, why don't you call and tell her? I need to call Linda and see if she's up for it. Now you be sure and call your Aunt Maude."

"And tell her 'thank you.' Daddy, I do still know how to behave properly. Bye. I love you."

"Good. Right, Son."

He paused.

"And I love you, too."

And so I looked back out into the snowy night, and over the pages of the interminably boring Dickens, my mind drifted away to the city that care forgot.

I dialed Aunt Maude's number, thrilling at the sound of the old lady's voice when she answered, the rhythms coming across the miles from their source at the center of the known universe. I felt that immense love and *cherisement* for soil and blood that were *mine*.

"Aunt Maude?"

She asked with no further ado.

"Yes or no?"

"Yes, ma'am."

"Good, Sugar. We'll get to the details later. Tell me, what's happening in the frozen wasteland of the beaux arts?"

"I was down in New York not long ago. Let's see now, the Met was…"

"Spare me, Darlin, I'm not talking about what the Barbarians are trotting off to see or hear and call themselves cultured. Let me rephrase that. What are you doing?"

"In school?"

"If that's where you want to start."

"I'm doing a paper on the Dreyfus Affair, and have been reading Zola."

"Did I ever tell you I knew a man who knew him?"

"Zola?"

"No. Dreyfus."

"Really?"

"Yes. Back when I was young. Well, probably not that young, I guess. Not to you anyway. I was in my thirties and it was Paris of the Twenties. I met this fellow who grew up with him."

"What was he like?"

"The fellow?"

"No, ma'am. Dreyfus."

"He said he was nice enough."

"That's all?"

"That's about it. We never talked about Dreyfus much. We had other things to talk about."

"And that's it?"

"It should tell you something about life and historical figures."

"Which is?"

"Which is that if the people who grew up with them saw them as just one more human, then maybe we ought to, too, in retrospect."

"I guess so."

"You don't sound convinced. Have you read Proust yet?"

"No, ma'am."

"Read him. Then we'll talk more about this. So, the Dreyfus Affair. What do you think?"

"About what?"

"The Dreyfus Affair. What do you think about it?"

"He wasn't guilty."

"That's it? What did his guilt or innocence have to do with its importance?"

"Well, he was Jewish, and…"

"And what? Haven't Jews been traitors since day one? He was guilty from birth."

"You don't believe that!"

"Believe it? No, I don't. But I *know* it. And you better never forget it. It's a fundamental of Western Civilization."

"But he was eventually exonerated."

"Maybe."

"Ma'am?"

"Make the distinction, Sugar. They're two different things."

"I don't understand."

"Okay. Dreyfus was really a nobody. He was no Rothschild. No Warburg. No Disraeli. It was what the case came to represent that made the Dreyfus Affair."

"And?"

"The way I see it is that the Dreyfus *Affair* was the French bourgeoisie's coming to terms with the *égalité* part of the French Revolution vis-à-vis the Jews."

"And the answer?"

"I'm not writing your paper for you. I'm just telling you one angle. You come up with your own conclusions."

"And if I want to look at it from yours?"

"Read Proust. Then we'll talk more. Have you got a girlfriend?"

I was used to Aunt Maude's sudden jumps from one subject to the next, from the serious to the flippant. It was one of the reasons I liked talking to her so much.

"Ma'am?"

"A girlfriend. You know, one of those homo sapiens with different plumbing."

"No ma'am."

"Well, do you have a boyfriend?"

My voice raised.

"Ma'am?"

"A boyfriend. You know, one of those homo sapiens with the same plumbing."

"What makes you think...?"

"Oh, Chile, you don't want me to answer that! It'd take all night. Just let's say 80-some-odd years of observing human behavior."

"You think I'm queer?"

"Oh, get your feathers down, little cock o' the walk. I don't think you're queer enough. Or your sister either for that matter. That's why I want y'all down here for Carnival. I've only got a limited time left to try and undo some of the damage done by my blood."

She was laughing, and I found my feathers soothed.

"Sorry, Aunt Maude. I didn't know you were joking."

"I wasn't joking. I just wanted to know. I guess I found out, didn't I?"

"So you'll know. I have no boyfriend and no girlfriend."

"Nobody special?"

"No, ma'am."

"Not even a warm spot for that Levy Boy?"

I was taken aback, and before I could muster a splutter, Aunt Maude was laughing.

"Bet you would like to know how I know about that."

"He's married and having a kid."

"So."

"So, what?"

"That means he can't have the hots for my grand-nephew?"

"You sound like you think that's okay."

"Okay? I'd say the Levy Boy has excellent taste. Does he treat you right?"

"Aunt Maude! I told you, Mark's married and fixing to have a kid."

"Oh, so he's not treating you right."

"Wait a minute. I feel like I'm being accused…"

"You are, Captain Dreyfus."

"What are you…?"

100

"Moi? No, Dear Heart. There are others to do the slander. I just want to know if you're happy."

"Yes, ma'am. I'm happy."

"Then you're over Mark?"

"I don't know why you think there was ever anything there to be over."

"You don't know why *I* think there was or why *you* ever thought that?"

"I...I..."

"So. He did hurt you."

Involuntarily, I found myself feeling like I had to come to Mark's defense.

"Mark never..."

She laughed.

"Whoo-whee, Mon 'Tit, you're too easy! Get the feathers down. Now, ask yourself. Did you hurt him?"

"Ma'am?"

"Think about it. That's a two-way street, Sugar. How do you think he feels?"

"He should feel like a pervert for what he did."

"Good. Now we're getting somewhere. What do you mean, what *he* did? Getting in your pants or getting married?"

"Both."

"So, you didn't like it."

"No ma'am."

"And that's why you'll still let him get in your pants?"

"I won't."

"That's not what I heard."

"And just who...?"

"That's my secret and privileged information. You're just pissed off, Darlin', that he's married and you have to share him, that's all."

"And that's not enough of a reason?"

"That's for you to decide. You know what *I* think."

"No, ma'am, I don't."

"You ought to. You called me chez Maison du Turd, scene of bliss with Joseph Smith."

"We've never talked about that."

"Maybe it's time we did."

Suddenly, I began to understand her third degree.

"You know, I really would like to know the truth about all that."

"You and a lot of other folks. But the truth's stranger than fiction, even if it is a lot less interesting to the general audience. You'll know when I die how I got through *all that*, as you put it. I'm leaving my diaries to you. But right now, let's see if you can't come to your own terms with your own married man. Do you love him?"

"I hate him with a passion."

"But do you love him?"

"I don't know."

"You better figure it out, then. Life's too short. *Too* short."

"I don't know how I feel."

"What's it like when he's there with you?"

"What do you mean?"

"I mean, what happens when you see him, when he first walks through the door? Does a lump come to your throat? Does everything else but him go into nothing? Do your feelings just go plumb out of control?"

"Sort of."

"Unh-hunh. Non-committal at this point. Okay. Well, then, when you first see him, do you want him gone by whatever means? You don't have to answer me. You just need to decide how much of each feeling you feel, and come to your own balance. Just remember, though, he's going through the same thing."

Then, one of her conversation swings.

"Are you bringing anybody down with you?"

I was glad to have the break.

"No, ma'am. I'm coming alone."

"When do you want to get here?"

"When do you want me there?"

"I'm planning on leaving the Monday before Lundi Gras."

"Is the Friday before Mardi Gras Day all right?"

"Lovely. I'll get Harriett to make your flight reservations. I'll let you know the times. I'll have somebody pick you up at the airport with the keys."

"Aunt Maude, you don't have to go to all that trouble."

"I'm aware of that. But I want to do this, so humor an old lady, okay? Now, get back to work and read Proust. I'm going to want to read your paper on Dreyfus. Maybe it'll bring back my own *recherche du temps perdu.*"

CHAPTER 12

I suppose I knew deep down that something would happen during Carnival. Aunt Maude had not gone to all that trouble for nothing. Despite her marching to a Dixieland jazz drummer, she was nevertheless at heart a card-carrying member of the yenta sorority.

On the flight down, my first class seat partner was a chatty type whom I had to forgive since, as he had made clear, this was his first Mardi Gras and something he had always dreamed of. He was about 30, I guessed, probably a button-down type ready to get married, buy a place on Long Island, and have 2.2 children. This was his last chance to be in possession of his own life, living his own dream.

I smiled. A tourist full of images of New Orleans, which, truth be told, the denizens of the city would be more than pleased to fulfill.

"Your first trip to New Orleans?" I asked.

"Yes. Yours?"

"Oh, no."

"Are you from there?"

"No, but I've got lots of family there."

"So, you're going to see family?"

"Sort of. I'm staying at my Aunt Maude's place. She's refugeeing. My folks will be in and out."

He smiled consolingly.

"I guess that'll cut into your party time, then, won't it?"

"Nope," I said. "Add to it!"

He looked at me quizzically. I warmed up a bit, ready to engage in the openness strangers in travel have sharing intimate truths one with the other which they would never dream of mentioning in other situations.

"Well, you sort of would have to know my great-aunt. I strongly suspect she has a surprise visit from an old boyfriend of mine lined up."

I gauged his response. It wasn't exactly shock, but it was obvious that the comment was not something he was expecting. I laughed.

"Well, you *are* the one on your way to the city of sin."

"You're serious?"

"'Fraid so."

He tensed ever so slightly, and I couldn't resist going on.

"But, I don't expect too much. His wife will probably be with him, and with the baby on the way and all, I doubt even Aunt Maude'll be able to make the proper arrangements."

After relishing the effect for a few moments, I plunged on.

"Which is fine by me. The last thing I'm up for on this trip is a re-opening of that can of worms. I'll be satisfied just to sit on the balcony and watch the crowds. Of course, in honor of my aunt I'll have to go see the naked lady swing out over Bourbon Street. It's a tradition."

"Tradition?"

"Oh yes."

Another strategic pause.

"Back when I was about 10 my Aunt Maude took me down to Bourbon to see the naked lady. Mama had a fit, and Aunt Maude told her, 'for God's sake! The boy's got to learn sometime. You don't want him growing up to be a pervert, do you?'"

The flight was fun. I regaled the tourist with all of the colorful, bizarre, and seedy sides of the city told as those who know and love New Orleans are wont to do as much from the personal perspective as possible. After all, I thought, this was *his* dream, and why not let him know in advance that whatever it was he was in search of, he would find it.

I bade him adieu at the gate, and looking at the crowd awaiting the passengers, I saw the sign with my name scrawled on it. I walked over. The fellow smiled seductively, ringing my neck with a string of beads, handing me an envelope.

"Madame Maude was right. You are a hot piece. Your pictures don't do you justice."

I reddened, thinking, oh my God, what did she have in mind? I opened the envelope and read.

"His name is Etienne. Be nice to him. It wasn't easy finding you an available Creole this time of year, so humor an old bawd, let go, and don't be such a tight ass. Don't think about it, just do it."

I couldn't believe it. Etienne was smiling that seductive, sultry smile again. He *was* gorgeous, all right. He tossed up the keys in his hand and caught them deftly.

His smile took on a wicked turn.

"Well, is it a go?"

I stuttered.

"I don't know what to say."

"How about 'yes?'"

Aunt Maude's face, voice, and presence materialized, it seemed, there beside me, whispering in my ear.

"Why not, Mon 'Tit? It's Carnival."

I found myself repeating her, saying aloud ex corpus.

"Why not? It's Carnival."

Etienne grinned broadly.

106

"Allons, Allen!"

As we drove into the city, Etienne skillfully maneuvering the mess of traffic, I tried to figure what to say, what was expected of me. My aunt's "present" turned periodically to smile and wink, saying nothing.

As we entered the garage and Etienne parked the car, I came out of my fog. He held up the keys to Aunt Maude's apartment, and shook them.

"Do I give them to you, or do I go with them?"

"Look," I said. "I don't know what Aunt Maude told you, what deal she's worked out with you."

I was looking out the side window, consciously plotting escape. Etienne moved his free hand to my chin and ever-so-slightly with the side of his forefinger turned my head to face him.

"She told me to be good to you and treat you right. That's all."

"That's all?"

"That's all."

"And you agreed?"

"Yes."

"Just like that? You agreed to whatever it was that that crazy old bat suggested?"

"Ah, but I trust that crazy old bat. Don't you? She only wants you to be happy."

"And she's hired you to see to it?"

"No. I'm not, as you so delicately put it, 'hired.' I volunteered."

"Pardon?"

"Surprised? I know an awful lot about you already. You were treated badly and you're scared. You ran off and hid in your books in your garret. You're afraid to let yourself go, and if you don't learn how, it will eat you up."

He leaned over and kissed me lightly on the lips.

"And that's what I'm here for. To eat you up. So? Will you let go?"

He leaned back, gaze fixed on my eyes, his brows raised ever so slightly, questioning, waiting too calmly for me to answer.

"You're a pro."

I said it before I could check myself.

He took the bewildered compliment and answered with only the mildest hint of sarcasm.

"Sometimes, yes. And sometimes, no. Right now, no."

"Look," I said. "Let's go in and take this up inside. It's not that I don't…Well, I…"

Etienne was smiling again.

"So, I can come in, but just don't expect anything. Right?"

"Right."

"Okay."

He unlocked the door, and I dropped my bags. He seemed at home in my aunt's apartment.

He took the bags.

"I'll stash these. You mix us a drink."

He nodded to the bar.

"You'll find what you need. Make mine a gin and tonic."

He was gone long enough for the drink to get made. I handed it to him as he sat, well, slouched, back on the sofa.

"So, do I drink this quick and leave or slow and stay?"

"Okay. You're good. Another time, another place, and another frame of mind, and I'd probably jump at this chance. But…"

"But you can't be unfaithful?"

"No. That's not it. I'm just not…"

"Gay?"

"No. That's not what I meant either. I mean…I can't…"

"Shake what you feel for Mark?"

I froze.

"What do you know about Mark? What did Aunt Maude say to you anyway? My God! This is insane."

He sipped the drink.

"All that aside, you didn't answer my question. You don't want me because of what you feel for him."

It was not a question, but a statement. I answered it, I guess, buying for time.

"I didn't say that."

"You didn't not say it either. Tell me, are you going to spend the rest of your life denying yourself happiness because you can't work through what your aunt calls, l'affaire Levy?"

"I don't know."

"Well, don't you think it's time you found out? So, tell me now. Do we waste any more of our time? Can I not get to you because I have to pass through him first?"

I thought for a minute, looking at the intriguing, highly desirable, and willingly available man. He smiled again sipping the drink.

"Truth," he said.

I gripped my own glass more tightly.

"Truth?"

I paused.

"The truth is, you're right. I'm sorry."

"And when, my friend, do you plan to get on with your life?"

"I don't know."

"Do you still love him?"

I suddenly felt at ease with Etienne, as if for the first time I was with one of my own kind with whom I could be honest, with whom I could talk.

"Yes, I suppose I do."

"And it's keeping you from having any other relationship?"

"Yes."

"Then somewhere in there you still hold onto the dream you can have him as a lover?"

"I suppose so."

"Have you ever told him that?"

"The time is past when I could. Too much has happened."

"And? If you could tell him, what would you say?"

I looked at the ice in the glass as I twirled it.

"I guess I would say 'I love you.'"

"That's all?"

"That's all."

"So, why don't you?"

"Honestly? I would have to make the first move, and…"

He smiled, not at all coquettishly this time.

"And your pride won't let you."

"True."

He stood up, gulped the rest of his drink, and brushed my cheek with a light kiss.

"I won't try to compete with your pride no matter how false. But, I will say this, your aunt was, as usual, right. I'll go now. You've got business to take care of. My number is in the rolodex by the phone. Etienne Arceneaux."

He turned as he opened the door, smiled that wicked smile once again, and bowed in almost exaggerated form.

"Au revoir, mon cher. Have fun."

The door closed softly behind him.

I went to unpack, deciding that a shower and a nap might help me shake off the surreal nature of what had just happened. I wondered how Etienne had known which bedroom. He had put my bags in the one which had been "my" room for as long as I could remember any time I had visited with my great-aunt. We all knew without being told that this was a special place in Aunt

Maude's order of the universe. Other guests were put in other rooms. For some unknown reason, only I was lodged here.

The room was something out of an art déco designer's sketch pad. You expected Gatsby or some other of Fitzgerald's monsters to materialize at any moment. The walls were covered by all matter of prints and paintings from the old dame's days in Paris. Here and there were photographs of her with individuals who were a part of that life, but whom she would never identify nor offer any explanation for their presence in this museum of memories.

I was looking to see if perhaps I could identify the one who knew Dreyfus. One in particular caught my attention. I had never really noticed it before, but this time it drew me in. It was of Aunt Maude in full flapper regalia, toasting champagne in what appeared to be a New Year's celebration. With her in the classic arms entwined pose was a strangely familiar gentleman, a looker who obviously had eyes only for her. I smiled. Yep. I could see why he had a place on her wall.

CHAPTER 13

I was coming out of the bedroom and saw Mark standing in the French doors. I blinked several times trying to make the image disappear. It wouldn't. He really was there. I really was here. This was no flashback.

He took a step forward, then halted.

"Did you mean it?" He asked.

"Mean what?"

"That you loved me."

"What makes you think that?"

"Etienne told me."

"Etienne? Wait a minute. What the hell is going on here?"

"We'll get to that. Did you say it?"

I buttoned my shirt, looped a strand of purple beads around my neck, turned to the sofa, sat down, and looked up to where he stood just inside the room.

"I don't guess it would do me much good to try and deny I said it, would it?"

He still didn't move.

"But. Did you mean it?"

"I said it."

"But did you mean it?"

I felt the anger rising.

"Yes, dammit. Are you satisfied? I meant it."

He sat on the chair opposite the sofa.

"I'm glad. You don't know how much I've wanted to hear that."

He leaned back, keeping his eyes fixed on me with that look I recalled from the beach, only this time touched with a tenderness that I wanted, but wanted to destroy at the same time.

"But I hate you even more," I heard myself say.

His voice was low and soft.

"Why?"

"Why?" I spat. "My God do you honestly think this changes anything? Do you honestly think that I'm going to buy into this madhouse charade you and Aunt Maude have cooked up?"

Before I could check myself, though, I found myself laughing.

"Though one does have to admire the set-up. Only she would come up with this one. She's one for the books!"

Then, before he could respond, another thought came to mind.

"Linda?"

"Don't worry. She won't be in until Monday."

"During which time?"

"Nothing."

"And Sarah Jean?"

"We're staying with her parents."

"Oh, so you're not mine and mine alone?"

"No. Unless you want me."

"Oh, right. Social form. Cover all the bases, or do I get to have Etienne when she's got you? This is absolutely sick, you know that?"

"Is that what you think?"

"I don't know what to think. I need room to breathe. This is too much."

I got up and opened the doors to the balcony. The soft, warm, night air came rushing in. I stepped out onto the balcony, leaning over the railing, catching the eyes of a young man in the street, his girlfriend's hand in his. I took the string of beads from around my neck and tossed them down, smiling as he ringed them around her neck.

"Happy Mardi Gras!"

She waved a thank-you and they strolled on, arm-in-arm, she toying with the strand of beads with her free hand, and he proud of his catch for his lady fair. I stood several minutes allowing myself and my thoughts to become lost in the sights, sounds, and smells so unique to this city. I felt Mark beside me, his presence a part of the sensorial perceptions. I could not push him away any more than I could the swirling masses in the street below. He was a part of a whole over which I had no, nor wanted to have any, control.

He pulled me into his arms and kissed me. From the street came a chorus of falsetto cheers from a passing trio of drag queens escorted by what may or may not have been real sailors. Their Mae West-look-alike doyenne was aware that their own cheers had drawn attention from the crowd which was now looking up to the object of their joy.

"Go for it, girls! Look queer for the tourists!" She shouted.

Without even thinking I struck a pose, and, the eyes still on me, returned Mark's embrace, losing myself in the sensuality of the moment. A moment in time that was as it should be. For a short second "that other world" was the alien world and mine on the balcony, that of the drag queens and the sailors, and that of the gawking tourists was the real world.

Mark spent the night.

The next morning I woke to the smell of bacon and coffee. Mark was standing at the stove, dressed in just his gym shorts, his usually perfect hair now disheveled and the shadow of a morning-after beard. The slight "flaws" made him all the more desirable.

"Good morning, sleepy head. I thought you were waiting for breakfast in bed. Lightly scrambled, right?"

We ate pretty much in silence. I went back into the bedroom to decide what to wear. Mark came to stand in the doorway, watching me and saying nothing.

"Okay," I said, "I think I'm due some explanations here. How did Aunt Maude know about us, and why did she go to all this set up? And how does Etienne figure into this? What if I had...?"

I was looking at the photograph.

"One question at a time."

He came to stand beside me, his own gaze at the photograph. His answer caught me by surprise, his comment coming as a non sequitur.

"I see you've met Joseph Smith."

"What?"

He smiled.

"Joseph Smith, meet Allen Kramer. Allen Kramer, meet Joseph Smith."

"So," I laughed, realizing what Mark was saying, "at long last, a face to put with the legend."

"Yep. Does he look familiar?"

I looked more closely. I looked more closely at the man standing beside me. It was uncanny.

"You got it. Grandpa Levy."

"Nanh!"

"Yep. Now you know why your Aunt Maude takes such an interest in my business. It's, well, a family affair. Small world, isn't it?"

"She was his mistress?"

"Sort of. It might be better to call her the love of his life and he of hers."

"Then, why...?"

"Ah, my Little Prince, remember a Levy does not flout convention. He was already married, and had my father when they clicked, and in those days..."

I tensed.

"In those days. And today?"

He didn't speak for a minute, then continued as if I had not said what I had just said.

"Okay, that's questions one and two, how Aunt Maude knew and why the set-up. Next question, how does Etienne figure into this? He's one of your Aunt Maude's, I suppose you could say, adoptees. He is special, though. You'd be surprised who his father was. He died when Etienne was still a baby. Etienne's mother had been his mistress. He asked Aunt Maude to keep an eye on him. She has."

He paused.

"And what if you had've with Etienne? That would have answered the question of whether or not I was still special."

I let it all sink in.

"And you and Etienne?"

He grinned.

"Oohh! A little of the green-eyed monster coming to the fore? I ought not to answer that just to watch you tell off on yourself. But I want you and Etienne to get along and so does Aunt Maude. So, no, nothing like that. He's got his charms, no doubt, but," he pulled me close, "they don't hold a candle to yours."

Okay, so I'll admit it. It was a cheesy line, but it worked. And equally cheesy, I melted.

The next few days were as Aunt Maude would have wanted, letting go and not thinking about it. Linda came with a friend and was in and out, sometimes with her door closed, sometimes not. I asked no questions of her comings and goings, nor she of mine. Mark and I got together at his request at Etienne's place when he could, as he put it, "get away." I asked him no questions. Etienne had his own itinerary and nothing was said between us of Aunt Maude's set-up.

Among us all, it was decided that her house would be the best point of rendezvous for Mardi Gras Day. The place was crawling with people, and there were all the traditional foods. The significance of each delicacy was being explained to the "tourists" among us while we old hands secretly argued over not who *got* to, but who *had* to squire them down to Bourbon Street. The whole lot of us went to Zulu. Sure enough, Etienne's friend on one of the floats made sure he got a coconut which, with that most gracious bow and wicked smile, he gave to me.

"So you'll have a reminder of what you missed in case you ever decide you're tired of playing the role of mistress."

He looked first to where Linda and Sarah Jean were explaining to the tourists the coconut and what it meant to have one. Then, his voice all but drowned out by the cries of "throw me something, mister," he turned to Mark, the smile vanishing.

"And you, you lucky bastard, I hope you appreciate what you seem to have gotten."

"I do."

Naturally, Etienne drew the lot of taking the tourists to the Bourbon Street drag show. He pulled me aside.

"Oh, Prince, you're going, too. It's as much your obligation now as it is mine."

I looked over to where Mark and Sarah Jean were sitting on the balcony chatting with their own guests. Etienne laughed.

"He won't miss you. He's in his element. Now, let's go be in our element, shall we?"

And so the day went. Promptly at midnight, it came to end, and the city went to its annual repentance for its excesses.

As they were leaving, Mark pulled me into "my room." A long kiss and a final question which I knew was coming from him, but for which I had no answer.

"When will I see you again?"

I pulled back, the magic of having let go now quelled by the bells of St. Louis, washed away by the sanitation department's traditional sweeping away of the debris of the party.

"Let's not ruin it by talking about that right now," I said.

He said nothing more, turned, and rejoined the round of farewells.

Mama and Daddy showed up early Wednesday morning to take me and Linda up to Ville Platte to spend the night on Daddy's new houseboat before we caught our early morning flights out and back to the real world.

I was back at school. The time passed in a blur really. I skipped going home for Passover, but even Mama seemed to understand that. She was able to put the right twist on my absence since I had a lot of work to make up from missing the days at Carnival. My teachers and the administration were lenient, testament, I supposed, to me being a "good student." Spring break came and with it the senior class trip to Aruba, with a day tour of Curaçao for a little culture before hitting the beaches. Though our tour guide was unaware of its significance to me personally, part of our tour was a stop at the oldest synagogue in the Americas serving the oldest Jewish community, the Mikvé Israel-Emanuel Synagogue, the sand-covered floor of which was put there either as a reminder of the days when Jews living under the inquisition had to muffle the sounds of their footsteps while praying in secret or as a reminder of the wanderings of the Jewish people. One of my own ancestors was a part of that community and his story told at our own Seders. I wondered what he would think if he could see where his progeny was today.

Graduation, the family came up for the commencement, a few days in New York, and then "back home" to the porch sitters and those steady, slow, comforting rhythms of the Deep South. Long discussions with Mama and Daddy about the letters of acceptance for college. I was tired of the North, the Northern winters, and the provincialism peculiar to those "good schools." California sounded good. So did Texas. So did a dozen other places.

The Young Levys' baby's birth was announced. He was named for two grandfathers, causing a spirited discussion on the porch between those who thought naming for a living relative was okay and those who thought it wasn't. The debate seemed as endless as the summer days and pitchers of ice tea.

A decision had to be made. Finally, throwing the major contenders into a bowl, I drew one to accept. Emory. Atlanta. And that's how the decision of where to start the next chapter of my life was made.

CHAPTER 14

Fall semester had not started yet, and summer was almost over. Rosh Hashanah was coming early that year. It had always intrigued me that Jews saw the New Year coming with the harvest and not the planting, with reward of labor and nature and not with the cowering fear of their potential caprices. But it was sort of difficult to contemplate harvest and renewal to the droning of the voices in harmony with the ceiling fan from the porch.

I went into the library to rummage for something to read to pass the heat of day. The tall windows in the room opened at a right angle from the porch, and I could hear as a backdrop the traditional early September ritual of hurricane prediction in which the daughters of Sarah and Esther cast lots in truly native Southern fashion. Each had her own "proven" method of forecasting the paths the storms would take this fall, and each was ready, willing, and able to recite not only her own observations, but those of an impressive genealogy of names of storms and names of ancestors.

I was paying little attention to who was *en klatch*, nor did I pay much notice when the topic began to turn from natural disaster to that of the more human character. Since Miz Levy was the absent Hecuba from this ice tea cauldron stirring, she was the liver-spotted blasphemers' target. I smiled to myself at the imagery which flowed with the conversation. That had been

Mark's analogy after he read over one of my school papers on the Shakespearian Jew.

Whether or not in synchronicity with the incantations from the porch I could not be sure, but suddenly I felt an immense anger at myself for allowing a pleasant memory of my time with him to surface. To cast it out, I found myself drawn into the particulars from the porch.

I recognized Miz Santo's voice.

"All's I can say is, y'all mark my words 'cause it won't be no time a'tall before that little show comes to a vain and inglorious halt."

"I'm afraid I don't know what you mean, Charlotte."

That would be Miz Klein, always the innocent one just passing naïve comments, comments geared, by the way, in just such a fashion to make imperative the telling of what everyone was just dying to talk about since Miz Levy couldn't be there. A command performance was in order. I could sense Miz Santo's busty deep breath like some diva from a Wagnerian stage.

"You know as well as the rest of us what I mean. That marriage is a business deal if ever there were. Mark needs a wife and the Hershkowitzes need money. I hate to be so crude about it, but that's what it boils down to in the long run. I know, Betsy, she's your kin, and she really is a nice girl even if she is a bit Bohemian. But all that means is that you know better than the rest of us the dollars and cents of it. None of us is rude enough to ask, but any of us'd be lying if we tried to tell you it's of no interest. The Levy Boy? We all know about his other life, and there's no need to act coy about it. Besides, it *is* a Jewish male affliction, it would seem, as well as a Southern one. So that's two strikes already."

Mama cleared her throat and spoke in hostess tone.

"Is anybody besides me getting tired of being out here in the heat and want to go inside where it's cool? I'm sorry to be interrupting what you were saying..."

She paused long enough for the others to voice their opinions on the proposed change of venue.

"Please do go on."

I smiled to myself, proud of my mama's tact and diplomacy, and contemplated which in her balance weighed more heavily on her as hostess, her need to defend the dignity of an absent party or the suspicion that Miz Santo's barbed wire web was spinning her direction. As the group passed into the main part of the house, I heard Miz Hamilton.

"Well, all's *I* can say is in the cute tuchus department, Sarah Jean didn't get gypped."

Another voice, chiding but obviously not argumentative with the content.

"Beulah, hush! You ought to be ashamed talking like that at your age!"

"Ashamed? Chile, I'm proud of it. Why just the eyesight alone to see it at my age is a blessing, and if the Good Lord saw fit to let me have it, then I don't think He didn't mean for me not to appreciate the beauty of His creation, and, Honey, let me tell you in case you aren't so blessed, that rear end is one of the most perfect specimens I ever laid eyes on."

Mama laughed, the relief that the conversation was taking a lighter turn evident in her voice as the party faded from earshot.

"Well, Beulah, since you are the self-proclaimed expert in that field, I'll bow to your greater expertise."

Miz Santo's voice was the last I distinguished. She was not willing yet to let her issues drop.

"...and I'm sure the next time he's over here visiting with..."

The voice became hummingly incoherent with the mention of my name.

My mind involuntarily brought to the fore an image conjured by a power all its own. I saw Mark as I had last seen him naked, standing in profile as the late evening sun poured over the window transom in the drapery drawn gloom of Etienne's apartment, the light casting its aura around him. Again I felt that "thing," that realization that if for only a split second in time he was the perfect man and I possessed him and he possessed me.

I shook my head roughly, frantically trying to dislodge the image from my brain and with it the elation that it had brought along.

I heard myself say to the fading apparition.

"You're an asshole."

I heard Linda clearing her throat. Startled, I looked to see her sitting on the sofa.

"I didn't hear you come in. How long have you been there?"

"Long enough to watch you float away into a netherland in such a way as to cause me concern for your mental hygiene. Are you okay?"

"Honestly?"

"Honestly."

"No. I'm not okay. But I'm not maniacal or suicidal if that's what's got you worried."

"It hasn't. But it's what's worrying you that I'm wondering about."

"Not worried, are you?"

"Not a bit. Just wondering. I know you're in control."

"Ha! Now that's what I'm wondering about."

"That's how I know you're in control. So long as you're not sure yourself, you *are* in control. It's when you start to be sure that the troubles start."

I sat in the winged-back chair opposite her. I motioned toward the living room to where the ladies had gone.

"Were you listening to them?"

"You mean the porch bunch? Yeah. Why?"

"When have you seen Mark?"

She eyed me suspiciously.

"They were up here about a month ago. I ran into him playing tennis. Why?"

I laughed.

"Ah so the third world weary back pack traveler is now spending her afternoons scantily and expensively clad au club, in search, we might assume, of a winning match?"

She laughed back in retort.

"If one must bow to the custom of one's environment, then scantily clad is the best way to go au club. And even if I'm not too sure about the sonofabitch, I've got to admit that the sight of those buns on a high serve brings out the Beulah Hamilton in us all. But why the interest in Mark's golden boy comings and goings?"

"Because…"

I realized now that nothing would ever be the same with me. Not with my family. And not with my society around me. I would always be an outsider looking in.

"Because I love him. I miss him. I want to be with him."

Linda sagged back on the sofa.

"So," she paused. "I guess this means what I always suspected is true. He did get to you."

I smiled.

"Yep. Despite all yours and Miz Edna's best efforts he did."

I softened my smile, I hoped, to a less mocking manner.

"And I'm glad he did."

I was surprised by Linda's next question.

"Then why are you calling him an asshole?"

"What?"

"That's what you said just a minute ago when you didn't know I was here."

"I said that out loud?"

"You did."

"I guess I just lost control, didn't I?"

"I guess so. Do you want to talk about it with Big Sis now that it's out in the open?"

In monologue I went over it all, the sound of my voice this time exorcising the demons of the fear of discovery, the walking on sand to silence those footsteps into a forbidden world. With each new topic I felt clean and washed of guilt. Linda's face betrayed no sign of emotional response.

When I stopped, story told, Linda sat silent for a few moments before speaking.

"If that's how you really feel, then why don't you tell him?"

"Are you kidding? He's off being...God alone knows what he's calling it. I don't want mixed up in his shit. He's plain sick."

"Who made you judge and jury?"

"You don't mean to tell me you think what he's doing is all right, do you?"

"I can't say. I'm not in his shoes. If I were, I might be doing the same thing he is."

"And what's that?"

"Trying to make sense of it all."

"By going out and fucking up somebody else's life? Make that two somebody elses' lives."

"Who says their lives are fucked up?"

"What? How would you feel growing up with a daddy who has a boyfriend?"

"How do I know he didn't or doesn't?"

"Oh, come on. You don't think that!"

"Of course I don't *think* that. But I don't *know* that. And what if I did? Little Brother, it's a hard thing this knowing what's right or wrong, normal or abnormal, sick or healthy. You and I *think* we're from a good, normal, healthy family, right?"

"Aren't we?"

"Probably. Probably as Aunt Maude would put it, disgustingly so. But take a look at what Mom and Pop turned out for offspring."

"What's wrong with us?"

"Nothing in our opinion, but that's hardly what others would say given our shenanigans of the last year or so. Shenanigans, I might add, which we have kept well out of eyesight and earshot of the lord and lady of the manor."

"Which makes it all right?"

"At least it makes it normal and respectable."

"So, what are you saying?"

"I'm saying you won't be the first little faggot to have an affair with a married man. He won't be the first married man to diddle a cute piece. She won't be the first wife to hedge her investment by looking the other way. It goes on all the time."

"It's sick."

"Yeah. And so is humanity, God's noblest creature notwithstanding."

"You know, Linda," I paused. "I do understand why though. I really do. And that scares me."

"Why?"

I told her about Bert and Ernie.

"And you? Do you see yourself as having kids?"

"Of course."

"And how do you plan to do that without a woman?"

"Pardon?"

"Without a woman. Without a wife."

"I don't."

"So, then, you see yourself as getting married and all that?"

"Sure. Some day."

"But won't you be doing the same thing he is? Won't you be involving a woman in your own sham? Won't you be doing the same thing you're condemning him for doing to a child?"

"I don't understand."

"Sure you do. You just don't want to admit it."

"But…I'm not…well, you know…I like girls…"

"And he doesn't?"

"And do what he did with me?"

"And you, I suppose, played no part in it. You yourself said you seduced him."

I fell silent. We sat a few minutes in the darkened study. Linda rose and smiled, speaking gently in parting.

"Think about it."

I did think about it, and for long hours. The longer I thought, the more I realized it was a game I did not want to play.

CHAPTER 15

Atlanta had always been for me a place you went through on your way to someplace else. Aunt Maude was close to horrified that I'd choose "that overgrown crossroads trading village" over New Orleans, Emory over Tulane. If I had ever given it much thought at all, it was the place Sherman burnt and Scarlet was infatuated with. However, it would be something new, close enough to get to family if I needed to, and far enough away to keep them out of my daily, or now, nightly life.

It was still the South, though, and we were still Jewish. Uncle Henry got in touch with his wife's sister's husband who got in touch with a brother there who owned a fourplex close to the campus, and, of course in no time, I had an apartment arranged "at a good price, in a good neighborhood." Daddy made sure I had wheels, not too shabby, but not too showy. There was the money ready, it having been put into "my" account from the day it was opened on the way back from the doctor's confirmation that Mama "was expecting."

The one time I mentioned working part time to help pay my way, Daddy had put his foot down.

"Your job is to study and do well. My job is to provide for you while you do."

So, I was being sent off to college "in the style to which I was accustomed" as they say. Linda, for reasons known only to her, had transferred to one of the local "good" colleges and, even stranger, had decided to live at home with Mama and Daddy.

We were sitting on the patio the night before I was to leave, the trailer packed and ready to start out before dawn.

"Tell me," I said. "Why in the world do you want to stay here?"

"I've got my reasons. And besides, staying under this roof will keep me out of trouble."

"Is it a guy?"

"Maybe. Maybe not. That's for me to know and you to find out."

"Aw, tell me. I won't tell anybody."

"Nope."

"Give me a hint."

"Well, he's not a nice Jewish boy. And we'll leave it at that."

"Is it a serious relationship?"

"Like I said, that's my business. But since we *are* prying in each other's affairs, why did you pick Atlanta? I would've put my money on New Orleans. "

"I think you already know why."

"Mark?"

"Well, yes. That was a good part of it."

"Why? I mean New Orleans is a big place and he's certainly not the only fish in that pond."

"Let's just say that the more distance I can put between me and his mess the better."

"You're still hung up on him, aren't you?"

I smiled a bit, not so much from the actual question, but from the comfort of knowing I had a big sister I could actually talk to about "that."

"I don't know."

"I'd say then that if you don't know, you are."

"You know I have every reason in the world to despise him, and still…"

"Do you want my opinion?"

"Yes."

"He was your first, wasn't he?"

"My first man, yes."

It felt strange to say "man."

"Okay, then. Tell me, how do you feel about your first girl?"

I grinned broadly.

"I won't ever forget…"

"Right. And you won't ever forget him for much the same reason. He will always be 'special.' Now, after her there were others, right? And no matter how you felt about them, they would never be 'that one.' Well, Little Brother, nobody along the way will ever take Mark's place there either. But, take my word for it, there are plenty more 'firsts' coming along, and one day you'll meet your knight in shining armor who'll take you off to happily ever after."

"What makes you say that? You know how little a chance there is of that happening."

"How do I know? Because I know you. You won't settle for anything less, and you won't stop until you find him. Or he finds you. You see, *your* prince charming is looking for you, too."

"And if we never meet?"

"Just make sure you have a good time looking!"

"And you recommend this from experience?"

She laughed.

"Indeed, I do."

"Ah, so you've now found yours."

"Like I said, that's for me to know and you to find out! Oh, by the way, Aunt Maude told me to give you this."

I opened the package, sharing its contents with Linda, and chuckling over the "necessities" Aunt Maude had "arranged."

There was a false Georgia license which we could only speculate how she had come by. It had the address of the new digs, and the photo even was just unflattering enough to pass anybody's inspection. There was a list of nightclubs "you will be interested in." Finally, there was a name of "somebody you will want to meet, and, no, not for 'that!' He will be somebody good for you to know for what you are wanting to study."

What I was wanting to study. I had decided on history and I wanted to focus on the Shoah. Emory was a good enough place for that. The course catalogue had a number of seminars on the subject, which stood to reason given that Jews were a considerable and prominent part of the student and faculty populations.

It didn't take me long, though, to back away from that group. They were overwhelmingly sons and daughters of Northeasterners whose mamas and daddies may have had the money to send their privileged progeny to Ivy League, but said offspring's academics and entrance exam scores were just below the high cut off for the "who, us?" admissions quotas on the Hebrew Children. Emory was more than happy to get them, their money, and their grateful parental endowments.

I just flat didn't belong in that group. They were way too orthodox for me, and I don't mean in the theological sense. I knew it was the shtettl mentality in a 20th Century American environment, but that didn't make it any easier to deal with beyond the abstract. They were orthodox whatever the subject, beset by group think, and possessed of their secret agents bent on hunting down heretics, ever ready for a secular bet din, and I suspected not averse if need be to a little pogrom action themselves. They had their *idées fixes* as to what being a Jew, a Southerner, a Socialist, a Democrat or a Republican, a Baptist, a Mexican, a frat rat, a debutante, or what-have-you was supposed to be, and that was that. Fellow tribals though we might be, the boundary between me and them was as distinct as the Amu Darya.

My class schedule was not particularly difficult. I seemed to be impressing all the right people, and I had time for my "social life." Given that the last thing I wanted was a "love" life, a "sex life" took up a good part of my free time, and the bar scene of Atlanta and the free-wheeling atmosphere which marked the years of the '70s was what, I guess you might say, "met my needs." There was a bar catering to whatever your taste du jour and I gave them all a shot, finally settling on my favorites. This one for dancing. That one for pick-ups. The other one for a few drinks just to relax among your own kind with no ulterior motives in mind. There were the cabarets where the drag queens put on spectacular productions that even the straight folks came to see. There was even a place where the politicals came together post-Stonewall.

I suppose I should have felt more at home there, but, politics and the liberation of the oppressed masses aside, I found myself most out of place there. They, by and large, didn't trust me, and no small few were just plain bitchy toward me. Why? They couldn't get past the image and the reputation I was bringing as my bar baggage.

I was too hot. It wasn't that I chose to be that, mind you. At first I didn't quite get it. I wasn't my type, but it didn't take me long to figure out that while I wasn't what I'd pick for a roll in the hay, I *was* my type's type. I'll admit it, I played it. But I played it in the bars, behind closed doors if you will. It bothered me, though, when I began to realize that I carried the image even when the attitude was far removed from that.

What do I mean?

Let me explain. I had made contact with the individual that Aunt Maude had recommended to me as that "somebody good for you to know for what you are wanting to study." David Fehér would later be my bona fide Gypsy prince and kidnap me for a spell and a ride in *that* caravan. In the beginning, it was an academic "professional" relationship. He had introduced me to his own area of study, the Porajmos, the Roma holocaust. I had scored something of a coup with a paper I had written focused on the outplay in his native Hungary, documenting the details of the distinctions drawn there between the assimilated and unassimilated elements of the population. Some of those documents he had translated for me, it turned out, put into question some of the traditional interpretations about this little known group of victims.

All that aside, it attracted some attention and, highly unusual, I was invited to read my paper. Great, right? No. The professor for whom I wrote it counseled against it. What? I mean, isn't just such…?

"Why?" I asked.

"Look at you. Listen to you. They'll not take you seriously and will pick you to pieces."

I wasn't following him.

"You're too good looking and that coupled with your age and that accent."

"My what?"

"No, listen to it. It's so soft and gentle. You're blond and pretty. You're not much more than a boy. They would only want to fuck you. You have no brain, don't you understand that?"

No, I really didn't, but I took his word for it. The reviews, by the way, were positive and, interestingly, my age there was also a positive. But that and the way I was "received" by certain circles did make me think.

Like I said, I knew I was "hot." I never had to go home alone when I didn't want to, and I could count on having my pick.

Since I didn't particularly have in mind a discussion of the socio-economic strata of Zimbabwe-Rhodesia, no big deal. But when I did, I often felt that, well, I had to be somehow more "whatever" than others.

It wasn't as though I hadn't looked at myself at a certain level. I knew that the eyes were on me on the dance floor. I had the moves at the pinball machine down pat. I practiced just the right stance at the pool table. I knew what moves to make sitting at the bar. I made sure the pants were just the right tight to advertise the goods, front and back. But, didn't everybody?

I knew I had miles of legs, a nice, tight, perfectly rounded butt, what Whoopi Goldberg called long, luxurious blond hair, a tight stomach and a well-defined chest which I worked on. I knew I had a well-proportioned aquiline nose, pouty lips, strong slightly cleft chin, and dimples which when I smiled gave me an innocent little boy look.

This was explained to me by one of the drag divas with whom, for some reason, I felt comfortable with his/her take on it.

"It's your eyes."

"What's wrong with my eyes?"

"Nothing. But they are very special and, frankly, they are your undoing."

"What do you mean?"

"Okay, what color are they?"

"Green."

"Are they?"

"Well, usually. But it depends on what color shirt I have on. They change a bit."

"A bit? The color of your shirt? You really don't know, do you?"

I did know they were often enough the subject of comment.

"Then, tell me."

"Okay. You know what they say about the eyes being the window to the soul?"

"Yes."

"Well, yours are the window to a soul which attracts, then scares the hell out of people. You have no control over them. I've studied you."

"You've what?"

"I've watched you and, yeah, lusted after you at first. But I knew I didn't have a chance. And then I watched you lure in your prey or turn aside the unwanted. Your movements never changed, always studied and easy going, but the eyes…they give you away every time."

"What?"

"When you're being light and happy, they're almost blue. When you're being what you want to be, comfortable with yourself, they're an enticing emerald green, then when you are ready to reel in your catch, they turn a dark sultry green. And when you're angry? They go almost coal black."

"And now?"

"Ah! Now they are that one that so scares people."

"Pardon? "

"I call them 'Jewish eyes.'"

"Jewish eyes?"

"Yes. There's a, well, ancestral sadness in them. Like you know too much. Like you understand it all and know there's no way you will ever be able to express it in words. It's as if you are seeing something only you can see. It's almost, but not quite, an acceptance of the fate of the universe…and a vulnerability which brings out the best and the worst in others. It makes them want to protect you or destroy you. And sometimes both at the same time. That's what scares people. That's why I said they'll be your undoing."

It was so strange listening to someone I had never really paid that much attention to off stage who had spent that much time watching me.

Why? What was it that had intrigued him to such a point? I was trying to find the words to ask him.

He smiled.

"So, why have I spent so much time studying you?"

"Yes."

"I've never seen anybody quite like you. You've got it all. Looks. Intelligence. Savoir-faire. Charm. Self-confidence. And still, there's nothing at all arrogant or conceited about you. You come off so innocently unaware and above it all. But, then, there is that vulnerability. Can I ask you a personal question?"

"Feel free."

"Have you ever been in love?"

"Not really."

"Your eyes are telling a different story."

"Okay, I have. But that was a long time ago."

"But you still love that person?"

"Not really. I rarely think about that."

"But when you do?"

"I…well…"

"Still have unresolved issues?"

"I guess you could put it that way."

"Do you ever see him? I'm assuming it's a him. Do you know where he is and what he's doing? Who he's with? If he ever thinks about you?"

"I only see him rarely, which is fine by me. I have an idea of where he is. I have no interest in what he's doing. I know who he's at least pretending to be. And I hope he's not thinking of me."

"So, tell me. What would happen if he walked in right now? What would you feel? You don't need to answer me on that, but I do think you need to answer it to yourself. And look yourself in the eye when you do."

CHAPTER 16

I didn't look myself in the eye as to Mark. But I had had my other questions about me answered. It made things a lot easier, at least in dealing with how people were seeing me and, to a greater or lesser degree, how to better navigate my world.

I went home for short trips, growing increasingly distant from the faces and places of my younger years.

My attention was taken more and more by my studies. I found my niche in the Hungarian Shoah, fascinated by its special nature, how it played out, the ghost of Mark making an occasional appearance when bringing up Arendt, court Jews, and how easily and with what facility Eichmann pulled it off. I was studying hard to master the Hungarian language. David Fehér became my tutor there, more than happy to work me through the daunting grammar of the textbook and showing the greatest patience and, yes, pride in my increasing fluency in the spoken language.

Our relationship slowly evolved from the professional-academic to one of friendship. As it grew, he felt more comfortable talking to me about Romany things. We would "go hunting Gypsies." In rides on the freeway, he would point out campers, buses, cars.

"There's one. See that patrin? They're…"

And he would name whichever subgroup they belonged to. He would take me as a guest to various get-togethers, concerts, and what-have-you, making a point that I was to be treated with respect and any questions I might have be answered honestly and straightforwardly. He was always off on some "Gypsy business" which he didn't offer any explanation for, and which I knew was none of my own business.

He was married and had three children who lived someplace else in another world in another life which, I supposed, were part of what he called his Gypsy business. When I asked him about that, he made it clear that it was an arranged marriage, that given his position in Romany society he was required to marry and have children. The marriage had been contracted when he and she were both children, sealed when they were in their teens, and the three children were born each a year apart.

"Do you love her?"

"You mean in the traditional, romantic sense?"

"Yes."

"Not really. That's not a part of it. I *like* her a lot. She's funny, a great dancer, a bang-up cook, and a wonderful mother to the kids. She makes no unreasonable demands on me, nor I her."

"And?"

"Our sex life? That was for procreation. Duty. Duty done."

"Is she...well, I mean..."

He laughed.

"She doesn't pry into my life there, and I don't hers. She's a looker and a healthy sort, so I suppose she has her opportunities, just like I have mine."

"What does she do?"

"As in work?"

"Yes."

"She's a music teacher."

"What does she play?"

"Instruments or styles?"

"Both."

"It might be better to ask what does she *not* play!"

"That good, hunh?"

"That good."

I tried to figure how to broach the subject to get an answer to my own quandary. Finally, I decided to just go for it.

"David, have you ever fallen in love with someone?"

"No. That's a luxury I can't afford. It wouldn't be fair to the other person."

"But what if you did? What would you do? How would you handle it?"

"Do you mean would I 'leave' Julia?"

"I suppose."

"Okay, this is just theoretical. But, no, I wouldn't. The other person would have to accept that there's duty and obligation with Julia and the kids. If she or he could deal with that, maybe. But like I said, it's a luxury I can't afford. Why do you ask?"

I felt comfortable enough given he had said "if she or he," so I told him about Mark.

"So, he chose duty and obligation?"

"I guess."

"Are you okay with that?"

"I'm not sure."

"Complicates things, doesn't it?"

"It does."

Not long after, he made his move on me, I responded, and our relationship entered a new phase. That lasted for several months, then it was time for him to go. He had to "pack the caravan and move on." He had taken a position closer to his wife and kids, his clan, and a professional move up. We agreed "to keep in touch."

No ill will. No hard feelings. Good memories.

I decided to spend the summer break back home to "get over" the break-up with David. It wasn't that I was having any problems. It was what it was. There had never been any expectations. It was an affair, a fling, no ill will, and no hard feelings. Good memories. But I did need to get away and back to where I had come from to get to where I was.

And besides, Linda was getting married. Her choice had raised a few eyebrows, especially among the yentas. He was certainly nice enough, a lawyer who had clerked for a federal judge. He had been recruited by one of the state's best law firms. But. He wasn't Jewish. When he came to ask Mama's and Daddy's permission, he had very little problem getting it. Linda was happy and that was what mattered most. When he told them that while he wasn't planning on converting, he did agree that any children would be raised Jewish. That was enough for Mama to fend off the blue hairs.

"It's not as though we've never seen a mixed marriage around here, now is it?"

I liked Mike. He was an easy going good old boy with one of those self-effacing senses of humor. He called himself "Linda's goy toy boy." Surprise of surprises, Linda had decided on a Jewish wedding, and the rabbi was willing to officiate. As it turned out, the wedding was promising to be the social event of the season. Daddy was quite the proud papa-check signer. Mama and Linda spent hours going over all the details, the guest list growing ever longer as they made sure that nobody would be left off.

I was helping them check off the RSVPs. There it was. Mr. and Mrs. Mark J. Levy would be honored to be present for the happy occasion. I looked at the return address. They were back here. Linda saw the look on my face, or maybe in my eyes. She took the envelope.

"You didn't expect me not to invite them, did you? Form over substance at all times in such matters, remember? Don't look so surprised."

"It's not that. I'm just surprised they're living here."

"Really? You didn't think daddy's boy was going to escape, now did you?"

"What do you mean?"

"The heir to the Levy crown?"

"I just never thought..."

"They've been back for about a year now. Daddy got him a job with the state, and she's in private practice. They've bought a house two streets over from his folks."

"Do you see them?"

"Oh, we bump into each other from time to time here and there."

"So, how are they?"

"I suppose they're okay. We don't exchange intimacies."

A few more trivial comments and then the subject was dropped.

Nevertheless, the conversation with the drag diva about unresolved issues of how I felt about Mark coupled with the "what if" one with David added to my being where "it" took place all together told me that, if I were ever to move on, I had to know.

The wedding was everything it should have been, a real Jewish affair. Linda was beautiful. Mike was the prince. A lot of mazel tov, chair dance, Havah Nagilah, hora, plenty of toasts, and enough to keep the yentas talking for weeks about who had had a little much champagne. I was one of them.

I had gone outside for a smoke and a breath of fresh air.

"Allen?"

I turned around, and there he was, like a bad penny. Without even looking to see if we could be seen, I grabbed him by the back of his head, pulled him to me, and kissed him. He kissed back, then pulled away.

"Stop. We're in public."

"How public? Aren't these 'our' people?"

"What are you doing?"

"Making a decision."

"What?"

"Do you love me?"

"You know I do, I always have, and I always will."

"Tell me something. When you're making love with Sarah Jean, do you think about me?"

"No."

"And when we're fucking, do you think about her?"

"No."

"So. You can make that…that…I don't know what you'd call it."

"Yes. I can."

"But you can be with her here, what was it you said, 'in public,' but not with me. Right?"

"Do we have to go there?"

"Yes. Yes, we do."

"You know why."

"I think I do. So, I'm the little, dirty, kept secret?"

"I never said that."

"You didn't have to."

"Okay," he said. "It's my turn. Do you love me?"

"If I'm honest, and that's what I want now, honesty. Yes. I do in a strange sort of way, but I'm learning how to separate that."

"What?"

"Just like you can separate your feelings for Sarah Jean from your feelings for me, I'm learning to separate how I feel about you. There's the love I felt in the romantic sense. There's that love

I felt for the man who brought me out. Then, there's that love I feel for a friend who will never be a complete whole. I can't be satisfied with loving just parts of you on a part-time basis. It's all or nothing. Am I ever going to have that with you?"

"You know I…"

"A simple 'yes' or 'no.'"

"It's not that simple."

"For you maybe. For me it is. So, is it 'yes' or 'no?'"

"I can't…"

"Yes, you can. You won't. And that's a 'no.' But I want to hear you say it."

"Then, no."

"Fine. Take care and all my best wishes. And I really do mean that. But before we part, I have a few more questions."

"Yes?"

"Is it true that you and Linda gave Little Levy the Hebrew name Neftali?"

"We did."

"Did you know that's my Hebrew name?"

"I did."

"And that's why you did it?"

"Yes."

"And you know what it means?"

"Yes."

"Then, I think you understand my decision."

I went back inside, leaving him behind. Tuna Fish smiled. I asked her to dance. Her mama and daddy smiled. My mama and daddy smiled. The yentas smiled. The rabbi smiled.

She whispered as we went onto the floor.

"So, you finally gave him the eight-six, did you?"

I looked surprised.

"You knew about him?"

"I knew it was a him. I didn't know who until tonight. You can do better than that, you know. You deserve it. You'll know when."

"I'm not so sure."

"I am. Now, let's party and put on a show for them, shall we?"

Finally, I felt free. If it happened, it happened.

CHAPTER 17

School started and I was back "home in Atlanta." It felt good to be able to say that. I was always a bit amused talking to folks. For my Southern friends there was no conflict, but for my friends from elsewhere there was, it seemed, always the question about my references to "home." There was always that "I thought you said home was…" They didn't quite get that thing that wherever I might go and whatever I might do, I would always have two homes. The one wherever I was resident and the other where I came from.

I settled back into the routine of classes, library, and putting in my time doing the bar scene. I found myself "opening up a little" and letting a few people more into my private world. Among them was the drag diva who had become drop-in company and with whom I shared "the tea" on this, that or the other new piece on the scene. He had laughed when we were talking and I told him he was "my first."

"Your first what?"

"Gay friend."

"You? Oh, come on."

"No, really. You're the first gay person I've known that I would call 'friend.'"

"Not Mark? Not Etienne?"

"That's not the same."

"How so?"

"Well, it's hard to put into words, but they…"

I paused, trying to find the words.

He smiled.

"You don't want to sleep with me is what you're trying to say."

The comment took me by surprise. It was something I had not really thought about, but on reflection I realized he was probably right.

He smiled more broadly.

"That's the way it is, Prince. Sex just fucks up the chances of a good friendship."

"Always?"

"It's been my experience," he said with a touch of sad resignation in his voice and eyes.

He almost immediately, though, added in a much more upbeat tone.

"But a girl's gotta not give up looking."

He glanced up to where the Zulu coconut sat in a place of honor on the mantle.

"Do you ever see Etienne?"

"We get together whenever I'm down that way."

"And?"

"And nothing. "

"No nasties?"

I laughed.

"Sorry to disappoint you, but no nasties. Just…"

He interrupted.

"Friends?"

"Well, I guess."

He laughed again, a belly laugh this time.

"You'd still fuck him, eh? Or him, you."

"Now that you put it that way. But, well…it might fuck up the possibility of a good friendship."

"Besides," he looked at me, I guess the word would be slyly, "he's friends with Mark. Right?"

"I guess."

"You're doing an awful lot of guessing these days. "

I guess I was.

His mention of Etienne, though, did bring up pleasant thoughts of New Orleans and reminded me of just how long it had been since I had gone down. Thanksgiving was coming up. I really didn't want to spend the whole break back home with Mama and Daddy.

I called. Daddy answered.

"Pops, I'm glad I got you on the line. Tell me, how hurt would you and Mama be if I didn't spend the whole of break with y'all?"

"Why, Son?"

"Aunt Maude's been on my mind a lot lately, and I thought it might be good to go spend some time with her."

"Well, you know how your mama is by her, but I think that's probably a good idea. Maude's not getting any younger and she's beginning to really wind down."

"Sir?"

"Oh, she's doing well enough. Just winding down."

"Will you clear it with Mama, then?"

"You bet. So…"

The conversation went to plans for the holidays, how are you doing in school, anybody special yet, you've still got plenty of time for that, do you hear from the Golden girl…?

I was making non-committal answers to Daddy's questions. Then his tone changed to the one which brought to my mind's eye that slight smile, but coded with it that what he had to say was going to be serious and would be a "that's all I'm going to say about that."

"Look, Son. I want you to keep what I'm about to say just between us for right now, and don't say anything to your Aunt Maude unless she brings it up."

He paused, waiting for my agreement.

"Yessir. What is it?"

I was prepared for some kind of bad news concerning her state of well-being, not what came next.

"Your Aunt Maude wanted me to know...well...about certain things going on in your life. She told me not to tell you she had said anything to me, for me to wait for you to talk to me."

He paused, I supposed, waiting to gauge my reaction.

"Yessir."

He continued with an obvious relief now in his voice.

"She said you would tell me when you are ready, but for me to talk to you and support you. I will. You're my boy. I'm proud of you, and I love you. I want you to be happy."

"Yessir."

"I haven't said anything to your mama. Maude made me promise not to. But I think you know your mama already knows. Mamas are like that. Don't worry."

"Thank you, Daddy. I love you and Mama so much. Thank you. We'll talk. Soon."

"Whenever you're ready. Wanna talk to your mama now?"

Mama came on the line, and as expected was let down that I would not be spending the whole time with them.

"Mama, you know I need to see Aunt Maude before..."

"Before your own mama?"

"You know what I mean."

She sort of surprised me with how quickly she changed her tone.

"Yes, Hon, I do. You ought to spend some time with her while you still can. I was just doing my role as Jewish mother."

I laughed.

"And you did it well."

"I guess it's long since time I cut the apron strings, hunh?"

"I didn't say that."

"You didn't have to. But you'll always be my baby boy."

"And you'll always be my mama."

When I called Aunt Maude, before I could even bring the subject of a visit up, she was on it.

"So, are you coming down to see Crazy Aunt Maude in the Attic before she croaks?"

"Aww, Aunt Maude, you know you're not …"

"I'm not what? Damn, Chile. Are you as dumb as the rest of our bunch? I'm closing in on 90, well past three score and ten and long since on borrowed time. But, no, Mon 'Tit, no plans on checking out just yet. It's too much fun watching the family fortune tellers laying bets and squirming that I may just outlive them all."

"Well, how's Friday after Thanksgiving sound to you?"

"Stay until Sunday?"

"If I'm welcome."

"You're always welcome. I'll have your room ready. Can I get your tickets for you?"

"I can…"

"Of course you can, but let me spend my money on something worthwhile, okay? And besides, I was already getting ready to have you down. I've got something for you."

"Not another of your, uh, 'presents'!"

"Oh, no. My sources tell me you're doing a pretty good job of it yourself. That is now that you finally got past l'affaire Levy. It's something else. "

"What?"

"Just wait 'til you get here, Hasty Britches. I'll let Etienne know you're coming. I know he'll want to see you. Anybody else you want to see?"

"No ma'am."

"Nobody else, then. Just you and Etienne."

Thanksgiving was all it should have been. There was a batch of pralines from Miz Edna for "my baby." Mike and Linda were there. It was nice to see just how well Mike had "fit in." He kept us rolling with his court room stories, one of which I suspected he had saved just for me. It seemed a rather prominent local lady had happened home and caught hubby in a compromising position with the pool boy and, let's just say the authorities had to intervene. To the charge of "attempted homicide," she had offered as her defense, "If that's what I'd had in mind there'd've been no 'attempted' to it. All I needed to do to straighten him out was to wing him. And I did. Besides, didn't I sign the check for the boy's severance pay myself? And ain't nobody moved out either, have they? As far as I'm concerned, this matter is settled. I don't know what the fuss is all about." Mike said the judge shook his head, cited the law, and reminded her that the state did, after all, still have an interest in the fuss.

When I got to Aunt Maude's she was as she would say, "all gussied up ready to get a po' boy at Johnny's" and go for a stroll around the Quarter since it was such a pretty day. Then came a request I never expected to hear from her. She wanted to go to services "to show you off." I know you're not supposed to think of services as fun, but it was hard to keep a straight face as heads turned and tongues wagged in whisper that "that woman come up in here at all, and much less come bringing in…"

Only at the recitation of the kaddish did Aunt Maude's amused air change. She began the recitation of the ancient verses, solemnly mouthing the words, but at the verse *b'al'ma di v'ra khir'utei,* she turned to look at me, spoke the words aloud, then went back to her faraway look and silent mouthing.

Back at la Maison du Turd de Vache, Aunt Maude quickly got down to business after fixing herself a drink and proffering me a joint.

"Ma'am?"

"Oh don't be such a fuddy duddy. I knew what this was back in Paris. It was a lot easier to come by then than it is now, mind you. But it's never been my drug of choice. I prefer my scotch, my bow to bourgeois respectability in my vices. Anyway, I understand from the source that this is pretty good, so be careful."

It was. I was relaxed. Aunt Maude excused herself and came back with a small, inlaid, mahogany box and a key.

"As promised," she said. "Just a little early. I wanted to make sure they went from my hand to yours."

"What is it?"

"Well, open it and find out."

I turned the key and raised the lid. Inside were packages of letters tied with ribbon, some photographs, and several small notebooks.

I smiled, my eyes misting a little, got up, and gave her a hug.

"So," I said, "*à la recherché du temps perdu?*"

"They're yours now."

Back in "my room," I fell entranced into this record of what was life for two Jews in love in Paris before a world disappeared, *temps perdu.*

For the first time since Linda's wedding, I allowed my thoughts to wander to Mark and "what if." Aunt Maude's musings to herself on being the "dirty secret" mirrored so many of my own, and yet she had decided to accept the role. I had not. I looked first at the pictures in the box, then to those on the walls, and I began to understand what Linda, Etienne, Tuna Fish, and the Diva had seen that others had not. I was not willing to have just a life of secret memories as the record of that part of my existence.

Saturday Etienne came for us to take Aunt Maude out to dinner, he having made the arrangements for Tujague's, her and my favorite place from the time she had taken me there for my first turtle soup when I was still a toddler, and worn out, and before I could eat my first bite, I fell asleep and into the bowl.

After dinner Aunt Maude insisted that we go dancing and "leave the old lady make her own way home."

"So," Etienne said on the way to his bar of choice for dancing, "what do you hear from Mark?"

"Nothing. I'm past that now."

"That's what your Aunt Maude says. I'm not sure he is though."

"Pardon? How do you know that?"

"Well, your name does still come up."

"So, you see him?"

"When he's in town."

"And?"

"And he still talks about you. He still has issues."

"Such as?"

"Wishing he could have been what you wanted."

"Well, he couldn't. He'll get over it."

"Maybe. Maybe not. Do you want to see him?"

"Why would I?"

"He's in town this weekend and knows you're down."

I stopped.

"Wait a minute. This is not another of yours and Aunt Maude's set-ups, is it?"

"No, not that. It's just that he's here. He knows we'll be going out together. He knows where I like to go, and it wouldn't surprise me if he, well, popped up. You know how he is."

"Don't I just. Thanks for the warning."

Sure enough, inside the bar, I looked out to the dance floor and there he was, strutting his perfect stuff. I was within slap-your-face distance when, thankfully, I realized the fellow dancing was not him.

Considerably abashed, when I got to the table Etienne was all but rolling on the floor laughing.

"Almost caused a scene, eh?"

"Almost. "

"You want to meet him?"

"Who?"

"The boy you almost slapped. He does look like him from a distance, doesn't he?"

I looked to the floor where the dance was ending. At a motion from Etienne they came over to the table. I looked at him and he looked at me. A brown-eyed-handsome man. There was a spark, no doubt. Etienne made the introduction.

I spoke.

"Are you Jewish?"

"No."

He looked quizzical.

"Are you Gypsy?"

His look grew even more quizzical with each of my questions.

"No, American Indian."

"Good. Are you married?"

"No."

"Have you ever been married?"

"No."

"Do you want to fuck?"

"Kind of direct, aren't you?"

"Either you do, or you don't, and there's no sense in either one of us wasting our time."

"Let's go."

And they lived happily ever after.

À la recherche du temps perdu? Carpe diem. L'chaim!

The End

Review Requested:

If you loved this book, would you please provide
a review at Amazon.com?

CPSIA information can be obtained at www.ICGtesting.com
Printed in the USA
LVOW06s0543070116

469602LV00001B/91/P